BREAKING ANCHOR

Geonn Cannon

Supposed Crimes LLC • Matthews, North Carolina

Published in the United States.

ISBN: 978-1-944591-23-6

www.supposedcrimes.com

This book is typeset in Goudy Old Style.

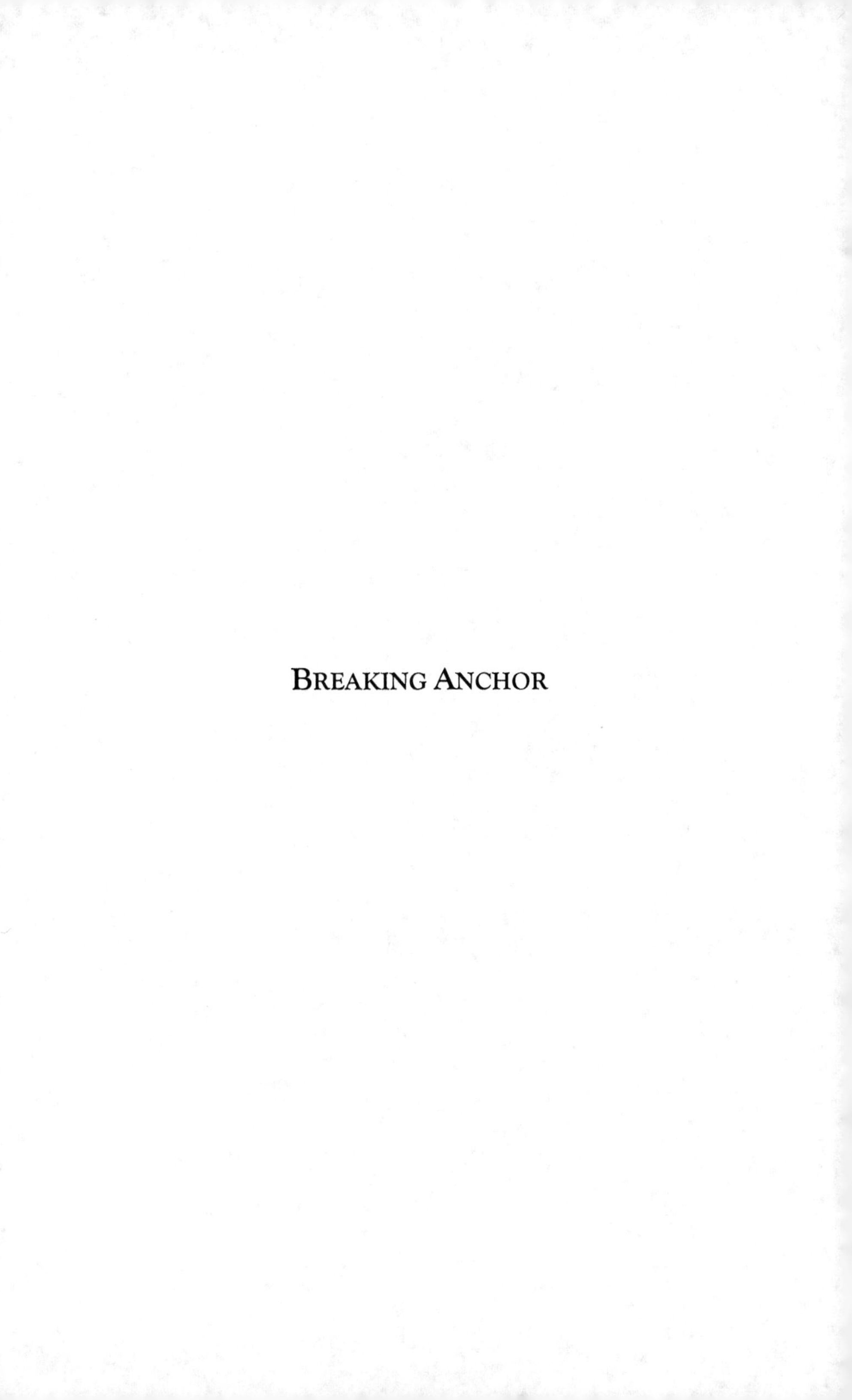

BREAKING ANCHOR

PROLOGUE

THE PAGES of the script fluttered through Sofia Kennedy's fingers as Sara touched up the blush on her left cheek. She ignored the sweep of the brush and the chattering behind the cameras. She squared her shoulders and faced forward. The cameras moved into position just underneath the clock showing the time in large blocky LED bars. The floor director held up one hand, counted down from five to one, and dropped his arm as silence fell over the studio. The music swelled and the lights came up.

Beside her, Del Stockton looked up and smiled into the lens. "Welcome back to KCTV Six News at Seven. It's been a fairly dry week here in Seattle, so let's head right over to Reed Joseph in the Weather Center to see just how long we should expect that trend will continue. Reed?"

The weather station was five feet to the right of the main desk. Reed Joseph, a tall and husky man stood in front of a wide green screen in an ill-fitting tan suit. He swung his arms and swayed toward the camera as he began his forecast. Sofia couldn't stand the man; he spoke in a booming yet monotone voice that made him sound as if he'd swallowed a bullhorn. She focused on the monitor set into the desk between her and Del to see what was coming up next.

A producer weaved between the cameras and dropped a freshly-printed sheet of paper onto the desk in front of her. Breaking news, fresh off the wire, to be delivered as soon as Reed was finished with his segment. She grabbed it, spun it around, and quickly read the text. A pedestrian had been killed in a collision with a bus on South Jackson Street. The victim was pronounced dead at the scene. They had a camera crew on the way and Lori, their director, estimated they would have live footage by the end of weather.

"...through the weekend. Sofia?"

"Thank you, Reed." Sofia turned to Camera One. The floor director held up a hand to indicate their crew had arrived at the scene. "We have some breaking news to report to you right now. A pedestrian has been fatally injured following a collision with a city bus on South Jackson Street. We have a crew on the scene, and--" The monitor above the cameras had switched to a live shot of the scene, and Sofia's voice died in her throat as she took in what she was seeing. A police car was parked at the curb. Uniformed officers were blocking off the street. But what drew her eye was the bicycle.

It had been moved to the sidewalk, lying on its side with one wheel twisted into an unnatural angle. It was green. It had a navy blue duffel bag strapped across the front of the handlebars. That bicycle on that street corner... that bag. She couldn't think of what to do, how to deal with the cameras currently aimed at her, the director who was now flashing the fingers of both hands to get her attention, but she couldn't think of anything except that bicycle and what it meant.

Del said, "We'll have more information as it's provided to us. We'll be right back with Evan Scott's End Zone."

The camera went dark. Del put a hand on Sofia's arm, just above the cuff of her jacket. "Sofe? What just happened there?"

The director had approached the front of the desk. "Sofia? Is everything okay?"

She pushed her chair back and pulled away from them both. "I need a minute."

"We're back in forty-five," the director said.

"I need a minute," she repeated, already halfway around the backdrop. She walked quickly past the large windows looking out onto the street and down the shining corridor to her desk. Everyone she saw stared at her, knowing she should have been on the set, but she couldn't spare a second to acknowledge them. Her hands were shaking as she moved down the row of cubicles until she reached her desk. She grabbed her phone off the charger, dialed the first number on her contact list, and began to pace. She could take three steps before she had to turn around and go the other way.

"Answer, Reggie. Pick up your damn phone for once. Answer. Answer."

The TV in the corner of the bullpen was tuned to the broadcast. When the commercial break ended, they came back to the live shot of the accident. Sofia watched as an officer crouched down next to the bicycle. She stopped pacing and stared as he unzipped the duffel bag and reached inside. He retrieved a phone in a bulky lime-green plastic case. He looked at the device, then touched the screen with one rubber-gloved finger.

The buzzing in Sofia's ear stopped. "Hello, may I ask who this is?"

"Oh, my God," Sofia whispered. She fell back against the desk and put the phone down without hanging up. She tasted bile at the back of her throat, the twisting in her gut threatening to push everything out. She was trembling violently. A producer approached her, mouth opened to say something, but he froze when he saw her expression. He brought his walkie-talkie up as he backed away.

"Del is going to finish the show himself, guys. Sofia's... incapacitated."

She slid down the desk to sit on the floor. She pushed her hands into her hair and finally let out the sob she'd been holding back.

Behind her, on the desk, the cop who answered her girlfriend's phone said, "Hello? Ma'am? Are you still there?"

CHAPTER ONE

Three Years Later

THE GYM wasn't the cheapest she knew, and it wasn't the closest one to her apartment, but Sofia chose to keep a membership there solely for its pool facilities. It was a beautiful pool, twenty-five yards long and ten lanes wide. There were windows on the short sides of the pool that looked out over downtown, and the room was accessible by a special elevator to which only members had a card. She was almost always the only person using it at four-thirty in the morning, alone except for the half-asleep teenager serving as a lifeguard, so she felt comfortable taking her time to enjoy a leisurely swim.

She stood on the edge of the pool and stretched her arms over her head. She began swimming when she was twelve, with dreams of Olympic fame. Practicing every day, building up her strength, and working toward the gold, quickly took over her life. One morning her mother parked outside the gym where Sofia would do her laps and asked her to wait before going inside. It was four-thirty in the morning, not even light out, but that was normal for them. Her mother was still in her pajamas.

"I'm willing to drive you here every morning until you turn eighteen," she'd said, "in return for being in the stands when you win that gold medal. I want that job, and I want to be there as much as you do. But honey, I also want to be sure you're still enjoying this. You used to love swimming. Now you treat it like work. If the choice is between getting to the Olympics and the love of the sport, then I think you need to choose."

In the end, she decided she just wanted to swim. Their trips to the pool became less frequent and more special. She stopped caring about her times and beating her own record and just swam until her arms were sore. She hadn't realized how much of the joy had gone out of it until she let it back in. Cutting down on her training gave her time to join the school paper, which led to a love of journalism.

Sofia finished stretching and dived into the pool. The water wrapped around her like a sheath, closing around her feet as she arched her back and aimed herself forward. She went with a simple breaststroke, frog-kicking her way to the other side of the pool. She touched the wall when she turned, pausing only long enough to determine no one had come in while she was underwater. She did fifty laps before she finally pulled herself out and went to the sauna. She stayed there for twenty-five minutes, then showered and dressed for work.

She spent ten hours a day at the studio, the majority of the time spent at her desk putting together stories for the half-hour (on a good day) she was actually broadcasting. It was a good schedule, with room for variety and spur of the moment decisions. Spontaneity was built in to her planning. If Katie wanted her to come out for a girls' night, she could work it in. If she wanted to spend the night at a sports bar, she could do that. She could go to a movie, add an extra nighttime swim, or take an hour to make herself a really indulgent dinner.

Sofia sat on the edge of her bed at the end of the day. The schedule had gotten her through one thousand one hundred and twenty-four days. Now, on the one thousand one hundred and twenty-fifth day, she debated her options. She could finish getting undressed, put on her pajamas, and go to bed. Or she could put on something sexy and go find someone to help get her through the night. She tried to avoid bringing people home if it was Reggie's birthday or an anniversary, but the current date was safe.

In the end she chose her pajamas. She didn't have the energy to convince someone to come home with her and, even if she did find someone desperate enough, just the idea of having sex was exhausting. She pulled back the blankets, set her alarm, and stared at the ceiling. Her curtains were open so she could see the light pouring in off the street, hear the sound of the cars pulling into the garage next door, see the occasional blinking light of an airplane or helicopter buzzing the skyline. All the life out there made it easier for her to forget how empty her apartment was.

The schedule also helped because it was full of things she'd never done with Reggie. The gym and the pool were new. The apartment was new. She was still at the same job, but Reggie had never been a part of that life. She wasn't trying to erase Reggie; she was only trying to ensure she didn't spot any landmines that would remind her of what happened and what was missing. The health club on Market Street, with a sauna that would forever feel too empty to use. The apartment she'd eagerly sold for well below asking price just because she could afford to and because she wanted out as quickly as possible.

She lay in bed and stared at the ceiling. Bedtime was the only part of her day when Reggie threatened to crowd into her mind. She forced herself to think of something else, anything else, and held onto it. Day 1,124 was done. Day 1,125 was just a few hours away. She closed her eyes and hoped it would be easier.

They met on a rainy morning at the Olympic Sculpture Park. Sofia had just finished the morning broadcast, five-thirty to seven. She hated the position, hated waking up at two o'clock and driving through the abandoned streets to sit in hair and makeup just to read headlines to a camera until the people of Seattle woke up and used her as background noise while they got ready for their own jobs. She wanted a promotion to a better hour, but her predecessor wasn't showing signs of retiring any time soon.

She was walking along the North Meadow, the train tracks to her left and the hum of the highway to her right. Everything was blue-gray and dismal, but that was the type of day she loved the best. She stopped at the row of red chairs and sat down to look out over the water. She hugged herself and thought about being stuck where she was. She loved her job. She loved reading the news, even if she knew the majority of their viewers were half-asleep and preoccupied with other tasks. She was sitting at the anchors desk! That was a huge accomplishment, no matter what time she happened to be on.

A woman strolled by. She was wearing a heavy Army surplus jacket over a ruffled tuxedo shirt and black trousers with a satin stripe down the sides. Her hair was cut short, shaved at the sides, and she had her hands in her pockets. She smiled at Sofia as she passed, and Sofia smiled back. She would never know why she said something, why she didn't just let it go as she did with countless other micro-interactions during the day, but she looked at the woman's back and raised her voice to be sure she was heard.

"Looking for a wedding?"

The woman glanced over her shoulder. "Why? You offering?" The woman kept walking for a few paces but then stopped. She turned to face Sofia again. "What if this is how we meet?"

Sofia furrowed her brow. "What?"

"What if, years from now, when our grandkids ask how we met, this is the story we tell. You looking sad and gorgeous in the rain, like you were just waiting for someone to save you. Me, dressed in a tuxedo. As far as meet-cutes go, it's a pretty good one."

Sofia laughed and stood up. "I guess so." She turned and started to walk in the opposite direction.

The other woman lifted her voice. "And this is where we laugh and laugh at the fact you almost walked away without even telling me your name."

Sofia stopped, grinning despite herself. It was a pretty good story, she had to admit. She turned around again. "Sofia."

"Hi, Sofia. I'm Reggie."

"Hi. Why are you wearing a tuxedo at seven in the morning?"

"That's another good story. Have you had breakfast yet?"

Sofia said, "No, actually. I haven't."

"I know a place."

She started walking again. After a moment, Sofia followed. They had breakfast. Reggie shared the story of the tuxedo, which lasted longer than the rain. When they finished up, arguing amicably over the bill, the sun had broken through the clouds to reflect off puddles and rain-speckled cars in the diner parking lot. In the end Sofia let Reggie pay in exchange for having dinner together at some point.

"It would have to be an early dinner. Maybe lunch. I tend to go to bed really early."

"Yeah? What do you do?"

"I'm an anchor at Six News Morning Edition."

Reggie raised her eyebrows. "Wow. I had no idea I was sitting across from a celebrity."

"You're definitely not. I said Morning Edition. That means when everyone else in the world is asleep or making breakfast or wrangling their kids."

"Not *everyone*." Reggie straightened and twisted in the booth to scan the dining room. She gestured for the waitress.

"Everything okay, hon?"

Reggie said, "Everything's perfect. Do you know who this is?"

The waitress looked at Sofia. "Um..." Recognition dawned on her features. "Oh! Oh, my goodness, Sofia Kennedy. I knew I recognized you! Gosh, you look so different in person! We watch you every morning in here." She picked up the receipt. "Let me take care of this for you, hon. On the house!"

"Oh, that's not~"

"Don't be silly! Although, could I ask for a picture with our cook? He has a bit of a crush on you."

"Uh... sure, absolutely. Yeah."

"Fantastic. I'll be right back."

She hurried off and Reggie winced apologetically. "Sorry. I didn't think you'd get roped into anything like that."

"It's okay. It's the intent that counts, right? I appreciate the effort. You've managed to make what would have been a depressing morning into something better. I owe you more than a dinner for that."

Reggie planted her elbow on the table and rested her chin on her knuckles. "We'll see how dinner goes and negotiate from there."

Sofia chuckled nervously at the open suggestion in Reggie's eyes, knowing that her cheeks had become pink at the thought. When the waitress returned with the cook, Sofia took photos and signed autographs for a few minutes before she begged off. She and Reggie left together, but Reggie had to retrieve her bicycle and Sofia's car was still near the park. They exchanged numbers and went their separate ways.

Sofia woke and rolled over, smoothing her hand over the empty bed next to her. She recoiled as if she'd touched something hot, curling her fingers against her palm. "Damn it," she whispered. She sat up and folded her legs under the blankets. She checked the time and put her hands in her hair, sagging forward. Her hair, which still felt stupidly short. Reggie only knew her with long hair, black curls reaching the center of her back. So as part of her 'everything new' campaign, she chopped it all off. She moved one hand to the back of her neck and smoothed down the hair. It still reached past her shoulders, but only barely. It hung messily over one eye, a loose wing that could be tucked back over her ear when she wanted it out of the way. Reggie would have been appalled.

The schedule didn't work in the morning when her guard was down. Her brain led her down dangerous paths and lulled her into thinking everything would be fine when she woke up. But the bed was almost always empty and, when it wasn't, the person who responded to her touch was never who she wanted it to be. Who she needed it to be. She got up and dressed in sweats for the drive to the gym.

When she was setting up her schedule, she considered cutting out the pool along with everything else. It reminded her of Reggie as much as anything else, but it was the one thing she couldn't eliminate. She needed the pool and those all-too-brief moments of feeling weightless and disconnected from the world. She changed into her suit and dived in, immediately finding her rhythm and cutting through the water like she'd been born to it.

After swimming her laps, she sat on the edge of the pool with her feet in the water. She inhaled deeply to smell through the chlorine and chemicals. Swimming had always been the one part of her life Reggie hadn't taken over. Reggie couldn't swim and balked at the idea of learning, so even before what happened, Sofia had spent her daily swims alone. Now she wondered if that was why she only felt at peace when she was underwater. It was the same, unchanged and unaffected by the huge chunk that was missing from her life.

The elevator arrived with a couple in swimwear, and Sofia stood up and gathered her towel. As she left, the acoustics of the pool area picked up their whispers. "Is that...?" and "No, it just looks like..." She covered her face with the towel, acting as if she was drying her hair as she turned to push the button to take her back to the locker rooms. The door closed on their hushed debate. She didn't know how to answer their questions. If they'd asked point blank who she was, she might not have been able to answer.

Reggie Mitchell's girlfriend.

One half of a couple.

A person who found her person, who knew where she belonged in life.

She winced at that last one. Everyone was always talking about finding their niche. What happened afterward, when the niche went away? What happened when life forced you to choose a second-best option?

She dressed and drove to work. The Six News building was on

Alaskan Way, just a few blocks west of the Pike Place Market. At the ground level it was a non-descript grey building, but the second-floor studio where they shot every broadcast had a glass wall which looked out over the harbor. There was an open-air balcony where, weather permitting, they could do interviews or the morning show could have a cooking segment.

The newsroom had three rows of desks, none of which were positioned at right angles to each other. Some were diamonds, others pentagonal or hexagonal. Sofia had a large diamond near the middle of the center row, the heart of the room. The wall next to the stairs was covered by a promotional picture she and the rest of the news team had done a year earlier. She and Del Stockton stood back-to-back behind a silver number 6. Evan and Reed flanked them on either side holding a football and an umbrella, respectively. Sofia had arranged for a desk where she could sit with her back to the monstrosity. It was bad enough she had to see it on buses, she didn't want it looming in front of her as she tried to work.

She had just opened her laptop when Kathryn appeared and made her way down the aisle toward her desk. Kathryn Zachary, senior field reporter, solidified her position as Sofia's best friend by placing a cup of coffee from Street Bean on the edge of Sofia's desk. Kathryn was petite, though she never disclosed her actual height even to her closest friends. Her vast array of footwear added or subtracted an inch on a daily basis, so it was difficult to pin down the truth. She was a member of the Samish Indian Nation, and her thick dark hair hung low enough that it almost qualified as a cape. Sofia made an inarticulate sound of gratitude as she lifted the cup in a toast and took a sip.

Kathryn pulled a vacant chair over next to the desk and dropped down into it. "Six feet tall," she said without preamble, "face like he just fell out of a marketing campaign. Loves watching sports, actually plays sports, has a great car but doesn't obsess over it, and he can sing. I'm not talking about carry a tune in the shower. I'm talking the guy at open-mic night that everyone thinks is a ringer."

Sofia said, "Uh-huh. And...?"

Kathryn sighed. "He doesn't curse."

"I'm sorry?"

"He's not a religious nut or anything. He just doesn't like cursing. If someone takes his parking spot he says 'aw, shoot.' If he bangs his head getting into the car, it's 'buster brown.' What even *is* that? Is that a person?"

Sofia shrugged, using her cup to hide her smirk. "What's wrong with him being G-rated?"

"It's not a big problem out in the world. But when we're f-making love... then it starts to get a little disconcerting. And then it carries over. He'll say 'gosh' when something scares him and I'll think back to when he said it while he was coming."

"He says 'gosh' during his orgasm?"

Kathryn tensed and grabbed the edge of the desk, rolling her eyes back. She panted, "Oh, gosh... oh... my gosh... Katie, that feels so flipping good..."

Sofia laughed. "So teach him some dirty talk."

"I've tried. He refuses to sense the tone. I'm over there giving him a full-fledged HBO special and he's giving me Mister Rogers. It's a definite mood killer. But how do you dump a guy because he's not vulgar enough?"

"Just tell him you feel poopy, but you need to find someone whose tally whacker will treat your flower right."

Kathryn snorted. "Sure. What about you? Anything to report?"

"Nope."

Kathryn tilted her head to the side. "Not even a fling?"

"No time."

"It's getting pathetic, Sofe. These are your prime dating years. Pretty soon all you'll be able to get are young frat boys who want to work out their mommy issues. Let me help you out."

"I'm doing fine."

Kathryn said, "Sure. I worry about you. Forget about finding someone. Let me take you out some night and we'll just get nuts. Drinks, dancing, drugs." Sofia raised an eyebrow. "Fine, no drugs. But drinks for sure. We'll even go to a club where you might run into someone."

"I don't want to run into someone."

"Okay. Fine. It'll just be me and you." She reached over and patted Sofia's hand. "I have to go. We'll choose a night."

Sofia nodded. Kathryn stood up, bent down to kiss the top of Sofia's head, and hurried off. "Don't back out on me, Sofe. Sometime in the next two weeks or I'm abducting you."

Sofia waved her away and picked up her phone. She had an hour until the morning meeting and no stories to pitch for that night's broadcast. There was an entire Back-Up segment fully edited and ready to go as soon as they had time to air it. Back-Up was a community outreach program she'd started when she was first promoted to the lead anchor position. People would call in if they had trouble with landlords, contractors, repair shops, et cetera. Basically any time someone thought they were being screwed over, they called in a report and Sofia checked it out. She loved helping people out, standing up for the little guy.

She kept the Back-Up segment in mind as... well, as backup. If she didn't find anything worth pursuing, she would suggest fitting it in just before Weather. She picked up the phone and dialed her first source to see if he had any leads worth pursuing.

CHAPTER TWO

MARION VOGT mentally compared each job to a time bomb. There were duties that had to be performed, a deadline which absolutely could not be reached, and disaster could only be avoided by a strict adherence to the schedule set forth at the beginning of the day. She owned Beacon Craft & Catering Services but, due to one team leader on maternity leave and the other just not showing up, she was in the field wrangling her people for the duration of the event. Today they were in charge of refreshments for the Perez wedding reception at Columbia Community Center.

Their van was parked at the service entrance and she had five waiters at her disposal. They were all wearing black shirts with white ties to make them stand out from the guests. Marion's wavy blonde hair was tamed into a Dutch braid. She was five-five with a face that had been described as 'adorable' from the time she was five, but she also had enough muscle tone from eight years of softball that no one looked at her as a pushover. She could stare down any man who worked for her, even Shaun Bryant, who had been recruited by the Seahawks before blowing out his knee. She was tough enough that no one tried to take advantage of her, but she made sure her employees knew they could count on her in a pinch.

She did a quick run through the event to make sure every drink seemed appropriately full. They had strict instructions from the father of the bride that the cake would come out precisely at three-twenty. She didn't know the reasoning behind the odd timing, but she considered it gospel. The client's word was gold; it didn't have to make sense.

Tanya caught up with her at the kitchen door. "We're running low on the lobster rolls."

"Ben should have put the extras in the freezer when we arrived. If they aren't there, substitute chicken satay."

Tanya nodded and headed off. Marion went into the kitchen and examined the prep area. Everything was where it should be, the trays full of appetizers ready to be taken out, and the cake was a beautiful centerpiece on the main table. She allowed herself to relax as she checked her watch. Kevin passed by on his way back out with another tray and she stopped him. "I'm going to step outside for some air. I'll be back in time to deliver the cake."

"Sure thing."

She went through the kitchen to the service entrance. Back in the day, when she was one of the waiters, she would have had a pack of cigarettes to occupy her break. Now she supposed the smartphone served the "something to do with my hands" requirement of relaxation. As she stepped outside she saw that a light drizzle had started. She leaned against the wall, one foot crossed over the other, and took out her phone. A small envelope image told her she had unread email, so she opened it and furrowed her brow as she read the subject. "Unhappy client. Your immediate response is appreciated." She thought it was spam, but the sender's address was vaguely familiar to her.

"Miss Vogt. My name is Samuel Flynn. My company hired BCCS for an end-of-quarter party at our offices..." She read on. The company was called K21 Solutions, an equity company. She remembered the party from six or eight weeks earlier; a bunch of men and women in ill-fitting suits standing around a bland sea of cubicles. As far as she knew, everything went off without a hitch. Their payment had gone through and there were no complaints. But now Flynn was complaining that people had gotten food poisoning from the hors d'oeuvres. He also claimed multiple emails to her had gone unanswered.

The service door opened and Tanya came out. "Miss Vogt?"

She reluctantly turned off the phone and focused on the issue at hand. "Is there a problem with the satay?"

"No, but the father of the bride wants to check in. He wants to make sure that everything is on schedule. I tried to tell him, but~"

Marion nodded. "Yes, I understand. Where is he?"

"I'll take you to him."

Marion returned the phone to her pocket as she followed Tanya back inside. The Flynn problem needed to be dealt with, but at the moment she needed to make sure her current client was satisfied. Judging from the language in the email he'd been waiting weeks to get a response. Surely one more day wasn't going to push him over the edge.

It was never in Marion's life plan to run a catering service. She originally took a job as a server because it seemed more interesting than working in a restaurant. At least with catering, she always had a different work space. She worked in penthouse suites, convention halls, and backstage at big concerts. She got to see the inner workings, behind the scenes where huge personalities like Dash Warren or the Femme Reapers became regular human beings trying to find the salsa. Eventually she was promoted to team leader, then shift supervisor. When the owner decided to retire, he gave her the option of taking over for him rather than selling to some outside investor.

The decision to buy had been expensive, costing her nearly everything she had in the bank. She loved the work, she loved the company, and even on days when the love was hard to find, she wouldn't have changed anything. She helped the crew clean up after the reception and sent them back to home base where they would package the leftovers for a local homeless shelter and clean all the dishes and silverware for the next job. While they took care of that mess, she focused on the email from Samuel Flynn.

Marion looked back through her records and found nothing to indicate he'd tried getting in contact with her before the so-called "final warning." She checked with their vendors and found nothing amiss. She looked up who had been working the event and called them all to see if anything had seemed unusual about the job. Everything came up with zero, so she replied to the email apologizing for what his guests had been through but said she doubted she was the cause. She referred him to the company's glowing record and lack of complaints from numerous other events around the same time as proof that their hands were clean, literally and figuratively. She wished him luck in finding the source and closed the computer, officially ending her work day.

She took the trolley home. Buying the company had necessitated moving to a smaller, less expensive place. It was little more than a single room that she'd split up using strategic furniture placement. She had a bed and a kitchen, a place to watch TV, and a bathtub almost large enough to stretch out in. She treated herself to a long soak and changed into a pair of briefs and a sleeveless T-shirt. The large picture window across from her bed provided a view of the street and the viaduct beyond it.

Marion turned on music and sat cross-legged on her mattress. She was in the middle of a great new book, and she wanted to read a chapter before turning in for the night. The window was open just enough to let in a post-rain breeze. It wasn't the life she would have chosen for herself or dreamt about as a kid, but it was spectacular. She knew people would kill for an apartment this size or a job they loved at a successful company. She knew she didn't have anything to complain about.

She took out her phone and opened the MEOW app. "Meet Eligible, Outstanding Women" was a bit of a misnomer, but the results weren't much worse than what she'd get at the bar on any given night. Only one new message from a woman who lived in Vancouver. She didn't specify Washington or British Columbia, but either way it was too far to consider. She searched around for a bit, passing on more than she clicked. Halfway through the search, her mood curdled.

"Oh, hello, Melissa." She aggressively slid her finger across the screen, dismissing the glamour shot of her toxic ex. There needed to be some kind of filter on the app, a way to ensure anyone she'd ever caught between the thighs of her next-door neighbor would automatically get trashed. She sighed and fell back, holding the phone above her head to keep skimming. This one was very pretty, but her job was far too demanding for a relationship. Maybe a one-night stand? That one was attractive enough, but she was a few years too young for comfort.

Eventually she got tired of shopping for potential dates and shut her phone off. She pushed herself up on her elbows and looked out the window. She could put on pants and a jacket, head out, and drag someone home for the evening. It would be even easier than the app. Just find a person with a good face and a serviceable body. Women at the bar this late at night wouldn't be interested in a relationship. She rolled onto her stomach and stretched across her bed to open the nightstand. Her vibrator was there, ready and batteried, and it wouldn't require her to leave the house.

"We have a winner," Marion said, retrieving the toy and moving up to a more comfortable position. She sat up against the headboard and looked out the window. She wondered whether people could see inside when she first moved in, but now she figured it wasn't worth worrying about. Someone in those other apartments might be in the same boat she was. Lonely, horny, looking for something to get off with before going to sleep. If they wanted a show, might as well let them watch.

She closed her eyes and imagined a sexy supermodel across the road sipping from a champagne glass. Unlikely, but who was to say impossible? Her lips curled into a smile as the buzz of her toy broke the silence of the room.

By morning she had forgotten about the food poisoning claim. There was no response from Flynn, so her brain focused on other issues. Regan Duffy was in concert that weekend and the record company hired BCCS to provide the backstage refreshments. Musicians could be their most temperamental clients, so she wanted to make sure everything was picture perfect well in advance. She took that job personally while keeping an eye on three other events they had going. By the time Friday rolled around, Samuel Flynn was as distant a memory as he'd ever been.

She took the trolley to the stop nearest their offices and arrived just before seven. She barely acknowledged the van parked at the far end of the lot as she took her normal space. It was the day of the Regan Duffy show and her mind was occupied with everything that would go into making it go off without a hitch. Regan's band had a full rider of the typical requests. She had everything in stock already except for guava and Green Machine juice, but she knew where she could get it with just a phone call. The rider also asked for "fish, as fresh as humanly possible," so she was going to send Maya down to the Pike Place to get the freshest salmon available for purchase. In fact, if Maya was going to the market anyway, she could also stock up at Sosio's while she was there.

Marion was halfway to the door when someone called her name. She twisted at the waist, keys still in hand, and watched as a tall woman in a red windbreaker hurried across the parking lot. The woman was being trailed by a paunchy man with a chinbeard. He had a camera hoisted onto one shoulder and he brought it up to aim the lens at Marion as they approached.

"Marion Vogt?" the woman said again, unleashing a microphone with a large silver six on the side. "Sofia Kennedy, Six News. I was wondering if you had a moment to talk with us?"

"Uh..." Marion blinked dumbly at the lens, her hand with the keys dropping to her side. "I-I guess. What's this about?"

"This is for the Back-Up, my consumer alert series. We'd like to talk to you about Samuel Flynn's company party."

Marion's brain began working again. "That's nonsense. I checked it out and double-checked everything. It's all fine on our end. If there was an issue with people getting sick, I assure you that it didn't originate from us."

She had moved toward the door, but Sofia blocked her. "You don't feel you owe Mr. Flynn and his guests an apology or a refund?"

"No. For what? No, we didn't do anything wrong." She managed to get the door unlocked. "I'm sorry, Miss Kennedy, but I've gone over my records myself. If there was any chance we were responsible then of course I would issue a full refund and an apology. But we are extremely diligent to ensure things like this don't happen. I didn't find any evidence to support Mr. Flynn's claim. If you'll excuse me..."

Marion had managed to get into the building, but Sofia was standing so that she couldn't close the door. Her right leg was extended so that the toe of her shiny leather boot was blocking the door from swinging any further.

"Why didn't you respond to the multiple emails Mr. Flynn sent?"

"I never read them," Marion said, not realizing until the words were out that she had misspoken. "What I mean to say is that I never received them. I checked my spam filter, but it was empty. Maybe Mr. Flynn was sending them to the wrong address. Now, I really am sorry, but it's a very busy day~"

"How many claims like this have you ignored over the past year? The past two years?"

Marion was so offended by the implication that she could only stare at the reporter. During that silence, recognition finally clicked in her brain. She normally wouldn't have said what came into her mind, but Sofia Kennedy had so thoroughly annoyed her that she couldn't help herself.

"I know who you are now. You're that reporter who froze on-air."

Sofia flinched. Her hand with the microphone retracted ever-so-slightly. Marion could see the real person behind the broadcaster mask.

"You freeze because some idiot woman didn't look both ways and you're out here criticizing how other people do their jobs? Really?" She pushed Sofia's foot away from the door with her own foot. "I did my job, Miss Kennedy, and I stand by what I served at that event. If you or Mr. Flynn have any other questions, you can direct them to my lawyer. Now I really do have to go."

She shut the door before Sofia could say anything else, twisting the lock for good measure. She blew the hair out of her face, shook her head, and turned to look into the empty kitchen.

"Right. Big day ahead. Let's get to it." She clapped her hands and began gathering what she would need for the next job.

CHAPTER THREE

SOFIA GOT back into the van while Harlan put away and secured his equipment. The damn caterer. It had been as if she shoved a knife directly into Sofia's gut and twisted by bringing up that awful night. She struggled to control her breathing before Harlan saw her. She didn't want him to see her red-faced and fighting back tears because then she would have to explain why it made her so emotional. Instead of lingering on the pain, she focused it into a hard crystal of anger. The bitch caterer didn't know what she was talking about, but that didn't absolve her from the repercussions.

Harlan finished in the back and climbed behind the wheel. He glanced over at her. "You okay, Sofe?"

"Fine." Her voice was neutral, emotionless. "How soon can you have that footage cut together for me?"

"If you want a rush on it, I can have it by tonight's broadcast."

She nodded. "Do it. I'll tell whoever is producing tonight to make sure there's room for it." Usually they waited until there was time to fill, but Sofia wanted to strike as quickly as possible. It was no longer about settling matters for Sam Flynn. Now she just wanted to see Marion Vogt taken down a few rungs. She looked out the window at the catering office as Harlan pulled out onto the main road. The rest of the day was going to be dedicated to finding every piece of dirt she could dig up on Beacon Craft & Catering Service to drive the bitch into the ground.

She made a gun with her finger and thumb and mimed firing at the front window. She began the Back-Up segment to get justice for consumers but now, for the first time, she was going to make it personal.

The Friday night broadcast was typically slow and usually allowed for a larger portion devoted to sports. Sofia asked for the time to include a special Back-Up segment and was allowed to put it in just before weather. She and Del covered the headlines at the top of the hour. During the first commercial break she relocated to the empty stage in front of a large plasma-screen television. She smoothed down her blazer and let the makeup lady touch up her color before the director gestured at her that they were coming back live. The screen behind her lit up with the graphics for her segment. The director did the countdown and the music swelled as the main camera closed in on Del's position.

"Welcome back," he said, "tonight, Sofia Kennedy's Back-Up was asked to look into a local catering company who, it seems, is serving up dishes that aren't so sweet."

Her camera came live and she nodded toward Del. "Thanks, Del. Beacon Craft & Catering Service is a small operation located in Beacon Hill, but they work jobs all over Seattle. They were brought to our attention by Samuel Flynn at K21 Solutions after the guests at a party catered by Beacon started getting sick. We looked into the allegations and uncovered this was only the latest in a string of disappointed customers who had hired Beacon for their events."

The camera went dark as the director cut to the pre-filmed segment. Sofia had dug up a handful of bad reviews for the company, a feat that was harder than she anticipated but not impossible. There were always disgruntled customers. During the editing process, she paused and thought about the morality of what she was doing. She was attacking this woman's business because of an off-hand comment. The comment had been cruel, yes, but unintentionally so. Then again, she hadn't fabricated anything in the report. She would never broadcast a lie. But if she happened to cut together a particularly damning account of Beacon's history... where was the lie?

At the moment her human heart was outweighing her journalistic soul. She would never air this report if she didn't feel personally affronted, if she didn't feel like Marion Vogt had sullied Reggie's memory with her callous comment. The caterer was arrogant, so positive she'd done nothing wrong, so dismissive of the idea that she could be to blame. If nothing else, the story would make her think about her business practices.

The director motioned to her that she had five seconds before going live again. She squared her shoulders and faced the camera.

"When we approached Miss Vogt for a comment, she was less than enthusiastic about speaking to us."

They cut to the footage: Marion Vogt, red-faced and huffing as she unlocked the side door. Her hair was sticking out from either side of her cap, her brow was furrowed, and her face was shiny with sweat. She looked as if she'd just run ten blocks. Marion's own voice came from off-camera.

"*You don't feel you owe Mr. Flynn and his guests an apology or a refund?*"

"No."

A quick cut to Marion trying to close the door. Sofia had stepped forward to keep it from shutting on her. "*Why didn't you respond to the multiple emails Mr. Flynn sent?*"

Marion rolled her eyes quickly. "*I never read them.*"

The rest of the audio was muted for Sofia's recorded voiceover. "With Miss Vogt refusing to even acknowledge there's a problem, there seems to be little chance for a bright conclusion to this story." On the screen behind her, Marion Vogt pulled the door shut. The image switched to the Back-Up graphic as Sofia took over live. "We'll keep you updated if there's any progress on this story, but for now Samuel Flynn, along with a lot of other customers of Beacon Craft and Catering Services, are only left with a bad taste in their mouths. Del?"

"Thanks, Sofia."

He read the intro to the next segment as Sofia stepped to one side of the camera. The director had moved off to coach Del, leaving Sofia alone in her dark little corner of the studio. She didn't have to be back at the desk until after the next commercial break, which gave her two minutes and thirty-four seconds of leeway. She retrieved a water bottle and cracked the top to take a long swallow. Evan Scott passed her on his way to the sports zone.

"Kind of harsh on that caterer, weren't you?"

Sofia shrugged. "I was only reporting the facts."

"My wife's company used them for the last Christmas party. I thought the food was great."

"You also thought the Seahawks were going to have a chance this year."

"Hey, they got close."

"Uh-huh," she muttered. She made her way to the desk and took her seat beside Del.

He glanced over at her. "Nice segment."

"Do you think I was too harsh on her?"

"Nope." He straightened the papers that included last-minute script updates. "It just proved what Back-Up has been about all these years. The reason you've won all those awards. Don't piss off Sofia Kennedy."

She nodded. "You're damn straight."

After the broadcast ended, she was feeling energized and powerful. She felt as if she'd been in a real brawl. Marion Vogt's first punch had thrown her for a loop, but she'd responded with a knockout combination haymaker that... whatever, she didn't know boxing, but she knew that she'd come out on top. She was buzzing enough that she decided to go out and get a drink at one of her normal hunting grounds. Seattle had a good variety of lesbian bars, but she was loyal to Sea/TT/Les for its policy of anonymity. No one recognized her, just like she didn't recognize the musician who was as famous for her failed relationships with men as she was for her music.

The bar was fairly crowded when she arrived. She moved toward the bar on a casual trajectory, taking time to examine what the night had to offer, and ordered a drink. Someone had moved to stand beside her before the bottle was delivered, but she waited until she took her first sip before she glanced over. A bit too young, but not so young that she had to worry about being carded. A bit too butch, but not yet on the "too masculine" end of the scale. She had a broad, flat nose and a crew cut. The ear Sofia could see was lined with seven or eight small golden rings.

They looked at one another and Sofia smiled as an invitation. The other woman took a glass from the bartender, drained half of it and twisted away from the bar.

"I'm Max."

"Sofe."

Max took Sofia's hand, her palm surprisingly soft against Sofia's fingers, and guided her through the crowd. The bar had a small back room with couches and low lighting. The music was a little quieter there and it allegedly existed so people could have conversations. It was actually created because the owner was sick and tired of their patrons getting busted fingering each other in the alley outside. Discretion was key in the back room; as long as no one made a spectacle of themselves, no one made a fuss.

Max dropped onto the couch, legs spread wide, and Sofia sat down on one knee. She bowed down for a kiss as Max undid two of the lower buttons on Sofia's blouse and slipped her hand inside. She teased and tickled Sofia's stomach as their tongues became acquainted. Sofia reached down and guided Max's hand out of her shirt to the waistband of her pants.

"Not messing around, huh?" Max said.

"Messing around is for kids."

Max said, "In that case, c'mere." She rearranged herself so she was sitting up straighter and took Sofia's hips in her hands. She lifted Sofia as if she weighed nothing, placed her on her knee, and slid her hand down the back of Sofia's thigh to bring the leg up. Sofia figured out her intention and pressed her knee against the crotch of Max's pants.

"There you go." Max put one hand in the small of Sofia's back to lead her in a slow but deliberate rhythm. Sofia arched her back and kept her spine as fluid as possible, biting her bottom lip as she pressed down against Max's muscular thigh. At the same time, Max lifted her hips off the cushion to rub against Sofia's knee. To their right, a blonde was trying to melt into the wall while another blonde knelt in front of her, face pressed against the open V of her partner's trousers. Across the room, a redhead's arm was gone up to the elbow under the skirt of a trembling brunette.

Max had leaned forward to kiss and lick Sofia's neck. "You like that, mama?"

Sofia winced. "I don't like that... don't call me that."

"All right. What should I call you, Sofia?"

She closed her eyes. Cardinal rule at Sea/TT/Les. No recognizing, no teasing, no winks or nudging about anyone's identity if it wasn't offered up. Calling her Sofia instead of Sofe was a big no-no.

"Not that, either. Sofe. I'm just Sofe."

"Okay, okay," Max whispered. She returned her lips to Sofia's neck. She ran her tongue up to the earlobe and then back down, moving aside her collar to tease around the bra strap. Sofia became focused on her orgasm so she could end this ill-advised hookup. She squeezed her eyes shut and thought about Reggie. Reggie's own butch-but-not-masculine haircut, Reggie's moan when she was coming, the way Reggie clutched her from behind when they were–

"Oh, there," she whispered, hunching her back and dropping her head down onto Max's shoulder. She tightened her legs around Max's thigh and then pressed forward to get Max off as well. Max rolled her neck, her head on the back of the couch, and Sofia kissed her hard to keep her from saying anything else to ruin the moment. In her mind it was Reggie's mouth, Reggie's tongue, Reggie's moan slipping out when their lips pulled away.

"That was amazing," Max said.

"It was." Sofia brushed Max's cheek, disappointed by the fact the structure was different from Reggie's. "It was exactly what I needed. Thank you."

Max smiled. "No problem."

Sofia lifted herself off Max's lap. Their companions in the room were still going strong, and Sofia led Max back out into the main room to give them some privacy. Max bought Sofia a drink and said she would be around for the rest of the night if she "needed a ride." Sofia thanked her and went in search of an unoccupied table where she could drink in peace. She finally found a stool and settled in to people-watch. She didn't anticipate any further hookups, and she doubted she would take anybody home. She'd gotten off with a sexy woman and she'd gotten the upper hand against Marion Vogt. All things considered, it was a solid day.

She leaned her back against the wall and sipped her beer.

CHAPTER FOUR

CONCERT CATERING always meant long nights. Regan Duffy played until eleven, with an encore that kept her and the band onstage until eleven-thirty. Then they went to sign autographs before they finally made it back to where the food was so they could unwind and let off any excess adrenaline from the show. Marion and her staff were required to be on duty until the band left, which meant they could be stuck there until one or two in the morning. She told everyone working to be sure they took a nap in the afternoon so they wouldn't start flagging.

The band descended on the backstage area like a Viking horde, disrupting the silence with a sudden wave of noise and energy. The plates Marion had spent the past hour perfecting were decimated in the blink of an eye. Her staff snapped out of their bored thousand yard stares and began circulating with plates that were quickly depleted. Lilian was at the bar struggling to keep up with orders, so Marion sent Jake over to lend a hand.

Regan Duffy was the last to appear. She was a statuesque redhead, dressed in a blazer over a torn and faded T-shirt. Her floor-length skirt, striped black and gold, was split to the hip on either side to reveal black leggings. Her paleness was accentuated by her stage makeup, which also obscured the freckles that spread across the bridge of her nose like a constant blush. She was even taller than usual because of her boots, and she loomed above the crowd as if her celebrity had granted her actual stature. She stopped to hug her band members and thank them before she moved on.

Marion watched her until she disappeared into the other room. She didn't like obsessing over famous clients and thought she'd long ago gotten over it. After seeing Derrick Lao passed out drunk with a buffalo wing hanging out of his mouth, she thought the glamour was forever faded. But Regan Duffy was supermodel gorgeous with an immense talent. Just being in the same room with her made Marion feel like a teenager again.

A stressed-out woman with a headset made their way through the crowd to her. "Are you the catering team leader?"

"I am," Marion said. "Is everything okay?"

"Everything's fine. Regan just needs her special plate."

Marion said, "I've got it right here." She stooped to retrieve the covered dish from beneath the table.

The headset woman spoke into the microphone. "I'm sending her in with it."

Marion was briefly startled, but she covered it well. Normally she would have handed it off to someone else, but if she was being offered the chance to personally serve Regan Duffy, then she'd be a fool to turn it down. Headset Woman nodded to her and pointed the way, and Marion carried the tray through the crowd to the door where Regan had so recently disappeared. She knocked once as a courtesy and then stepped inside.

At first glance she thought Regan was sitting on the couch, but she had too many arms. Marion looked again and realized the rock star was sitting on someone. The someone was a woman with curly black hair whose face was hidden by Regan's shoulder. The mystery cushion had one hand under Regan's skirt and the other under her T-shirt. There was little doubt as to what was happening, even without the way Regan was rocking her hips and arching her back.

"Oh, Jesus," Marion muttered, averting her gaze to the covered dish in her hands. "I'm sorry. Your manager said... she... I knocked, but..."

"It's fine, sweetheart," Regan said breathlessly. "You can just leave it there."

Marion risked another look and saw Regan gesture at the coffee table. Marion quickly set it down, muttered another apology, and spun on the ball of her foot to retreat.

"You can stay," Regan said quickly. "If you want."

Marion froze. "I... don't think that's... uh, I don't think so. I'm working."

Regan sighed. "Pity. You can still watch, though. Right?"

Marion's cheeks burned. "Um."

"I've been onstage all night," Regan said, breathing harder now. "I obviously enjoy being watched. C'mon. What's your name?"

"Uh. Marion." She was still facing away, but everything in her was urging her to turn around.

"Hi, Marion," Regan said. "Watch this lady finger me."

Marion turned slowly. The unnamed woman was looking over Regan's shoulder, her dark eyes wrinkled with a smile. She looked like something out of legend, a succubus feasting on her latest victim. Regan moved her legs further apart, with one foot flat on the ground and the other knee bent so her toe would be pointed. She gripped her partner's arm and opened her eyes to look at Marion.

"You're an adorable little thing, aren't you? Those blonde curls. Big blue eyes..." She exhaled sharply and rolled her eyes back in her head. "Sorry. I just... I really like getting laid right after a show. When I'm still buzzing." She bit her bottom lip and reached back, flapping her hand until she found the other woman's head. "This is Tara. She's my hometown lady."

Marion started to nod before the phrase clicked in her head. "Hometown lady, waiting after I clear the storm, remind me who I am again, keeping my bed warm."

Regan growled and bared her teeth. "Oh, fuck, yes. Sing my song while I'm getting off."

"I don't think I know any more of the words... sorry..."

"It's okay," Regan said. "It's okay. I came." She had gone limp. Tara fell against the back of the couch and pulled Regan down with her. Regan seemed to melt against the other woman's body. She pushed her hair up out of her face and focused on Marion. "What was your name again?"

"Marion."

"Right. Well, Marion. I'll have to be sure to give you a proper hello before the night ends." She winked and then reached back to stroke Tara's hip. "I guess you have to get back to work."

"Yeah. Probably should. Thanks for... uh, not thanks. But..."

Regan laughed. "You're welcome."

Marion turned and fled before she could be enticed to stay for the second act. She nearly collided with Lilian on her way out of the room.

"Everything okay, boss? You look kind of red."

"I'm fine. Is everything okay with the bar?"

Lilian nodded. "Michael offered to give me a break. I was gonna see if Miss Duffy's minibar needed any refreshing."

Marion hooked her hand around Lilian's arm and guided her away. "You know that Amanda Palmer song, 'Do It With a Rockstar'?"

"Yeah..."

"Well, the reality is a lot more awkward than the fantasy."

Lilian's eyes widened. "You didn't!"

"No! Not... um... no, I didn't have se~" She cut herself off as someone passed within earshot. "Let's just say that I think Miss Duffy is doing just fine on her own. We can check on her later."

Lilian chuckled and headed off. Marion scanned the room and saw that her troops seemed to have everything under control. She told Lilian to take full advantage of her break and escape the madness for twenty minutes. She'd worked enough post-concert parties to know that their night was just getting started.

The party finally ended, the gear was cleaned up and loaded into the truck, and Lilian offered Marion a ride home when she discovered she planned to use public transportation. Marion finally got back to her apartment just after four-thirty in the morning. She stripped out of her uniform, showered off the day and the smells of food from the job. She didn't bother to check her phone beyond what she saw when she set the alarm. There were MEOW notifications that didn't need to be read just then, and email alerts that she ignored in favor for sleep. Whatever they had to say could wait until morning.

Because she looked at her phone right before lying down, she knew it was just under two hours before she was jarred awake by its ringing. She cursed and grappled for the phone, knocking it off the nightstand in her fumbling. She crawled to the edge of the mattress to retrieve it from the floor and, once she'd gone to those lengths, she decided she might as well answer it. She swept her finger across the screen and kept her eyes closed as she tucked it under her hair.

"This is Marion Vogt," she said, her voice husky and odd. She coughed and cleared her throat. "Sorry. Who is this?"

"Marion, it's Courtney. Where are you?"

Courtney was her right-hand woman, her second-in-command. If she was calling this early and with that level of concern in her voice, there was definitely a problem. Marion sat up and drew the blanket up over her body.

"I'm in bed. We had the Regan Duffy show last night." An image from her dream flashed against the back wall of her brain, but she shut it down. "What's wrong?"

"I got into work fifteen minutes ago and discovered we had five cancellations overnight. We've had another two since I got in."

Marion was fully awake. "What? How... have you contacted any of the clients?"

"I only had time to call one. Apparently there was something on the news last night? I thought you'd want to be informed when they kept dropping."

"You're right." She kicked away the blankets, already dreading the mid-afternoon crash she would be sure to suffer. "I'm on my way in right now."

Courtney said, "Okay. I'll keep working damage control. I have calls in to everyone who was working the Flynn job to see if there's any chance these claims are valid. While I'm waiting for them, I'll see if I can salvage some of the runaways."

"Hopefully you won't lose anymore before I get there. Thank you, Courtney."

"I've got your back, boss."

Marion was partially dressed before she put together Courtney's news and the run-in with Sofia Kennedy the day before. "Oh, that *bitch*." She finished dressing and hurried out. She couldn't remember if the trolley was on a ten- or twenty-minute schedule, but in the end it didn't matter. The car was approaching when she reached the stop and she climbed aboard. The morning rush was underway but she still managed to grab a seat. She used the browser on her phone to search for Sofia Kennedy and Beacon Craft & Catering. The first result was a video from the night before. She fished her ear buds from the pocket of her coat, plugged one into her ear, and hit play.

"Beacon Craft & Catering Service is a small operation~"

Already Marion's hackles were raised. The way Sofia said "small" was so condescending and dismissive. Yes, they had competitors who were twice their size, but they were cold and impersonal. Going to them was like catering from McDonald's. Beacon was small and intimate by design. They put care into their menu. To hear her pride and joy diminished that way made her face burn. She focused on the small screen cupped in her right hand.

"One reviewer called the caterer's performance 'unprofessional and brusque,' at an event where the catering team was under the supervision of the company's owner, Marion Vogt. The same Marion Vogt now being accused of making everyone at Samuel Flynn's party ill."

The only thing holding back her tears was the strength of her anger. She knew that review well. It was the first job she'd taken as supervisor. She had been unprofessional, stressed, overwhelmed, and she owned the fact she had been brusque. She actually snapped at one guest who asked when the canapés would be ready. She still heard her own voice in her head, saw his startled expression. "They'll be done when they're done, sir, okay?"

There were more quotes from other reviews from across the web. The food was dry and flavorless. Service was slow. Caterers arrived late. She could have explained every single complaint. She could have pointed out these were five or six disgruntled customers amid an entire website full of four- and five-star reviews raving about the company. But she knew it didn't really matter. It was painfully clear that Sofia Kennedy didn't want the truth; she was only interested in burying the company.

But *why*? Why would some journalist suddenly have a vendetta against some company she admitted was penny-ante? What possible reason could Six News have to take her down? Yes, she had some bad reviews. What company that dealt with the public didn't have one or two dissatisfied customers? She would be willing to offer refunds to anyone who asked, but no one had. Samuel Flynn was the closest she'd gotten. Maybe if his emails had gotten through, they could have settled things without the news getting involved. Now would they have to go to court?

She squeezed the bridge of her nose and dialed Courtney back. "It's me," she said. "Can you cover things there for the morning? I think I might be more helpful elsewhere."

"Sure. I'm better with this stuff than you are, anyway."

Marion managed a smile. "Yeah, but let's see you prepare a three-course meal."

"Hey, I can almost boil an egg without burning down the kitchen. Do what you need. The place will still be here when you get back."

"Thank you, Courtney. I mean it. You're a lifesaver."

"Don't say that until I've actually saved you. Right now I'm just a foam ring bobbing up and down in the water. Let's see if they grab it."

When they hung up, Marion checked her phone to see where the Six News studio was. She would trust Courtney to take care of the fires back at the office, but she wasn't just going to allow Sofia Kennedy to drag her name through the mud. She was going to fight back.

CHAPTER FIVE

REGRET TURNED her morning laps into penance. Regret for what she'd done at Sea/TT/Les. Anonymous sex was all well and good, and she usually didn't let herself dwell on it long enough to make it a thing. But she couldn't even remember the woman's name. She could barely remember what she looked like or if she had come. Usually she treated her partners better than that. Regret also crowded in about what she had done to Marion Vogt. The woman had made an unfortunate comment, unaware of how cutting it really was. She couldn't have possibly known how much it would hurt. And in return, Sofia had used her power to cause untold damage to Vogt's career and livelihood.

She swam until her muscles burned and dragged herself into the sauna. She could issue a retraction. She could apologize on-air and walk back the story until it only focused on Samuel Flynn's claims, as it should have done in the first place. Maybe she could contain the damage so the first report wouldn't be an irreparable scar on BC&CS's reputation.

It was decided in the shower. She would undo the damage she'd caused in a special follow-up to the first story. She would own up to her bias, admit that her own personal feelings had gotten in the way of the truth, and she would do everything in her power to regain the trust of her viewers. Not only that, she would give Marion Vogt a chance to truly defend herself against the claims. A sit-down interview instead of an ambush.

At her locker, naked and dripping on the tile, she could hear her phone's ringtone through the vents even as she dialed in the combination. Four missed calls, all from the station's receptionist. She frowned and answered the latest call.

"Hello? Susie?"

"Sofia! Thank goodness, I've been trying to reach you for half an hour!"

"I was swimming. What's wrong?"

Susie lowered her voice. "A woman is here demanding to talk with you. I told her you weren't supposed to come in today, but she insisted on having us call you. She refused to leave."

"What woman?"

"Marion Vogt."

Sofia grimaced and knocked her fist against her forehead. "Oh. That's actually a good thing, Susie." At least it meant she wouldn't have to track her down. "I want to talk with her, too. I can get there in about twenty minutes."

Susie sighed, relieved that the responsibility of shooing an unwanted guest had been taken from her. "Okay. I'll let her know you're on the way."

"Thank you, Susie."

She hung up and took her clothes from the locker. She hadn't planned to go into work, so she hadn't brought a change of clothes. She would just have to fall on her sword wearing the sweats she'd put on when she left the house.

Marion felt like she could climb a mountain and punch the sky. She'd gotten the receptionist to call in Sofia Kennedy on her day off, and now she had to pump herself up for what was sure to be a volatile confrontation with the reporter. She waited in the lobby, placing herself in a seat where she would see Sofia before Sofia could see her. It was just one more way to gain the upper hand. She was buzzing with adrenaline and ready to defend her business.

While she waited, she used her phone to look up more videos of the Back-Up segment. She was treated to montages of Sofia Kennedy ambushing people in parking lots, blocking their doorways with her shoulder while they tried to block the camera with outstretched hands. The more she saw, the angrier she became that she'd been on the receiving end of these tactics. She'd worked too hard to make a business she was proud of for Sofia fucking Kennedy to take it down with a minute and forty-seconds of airtime.

The door opened and let in a burst of cold air. Sofia Kennedy was almost unrecognizable. Her hair was wet and hung like seaweed, leaving smudges of moisture on the shoulders of her oversized sweatshirt. Marion stood up and fell into step behind her. Sofia stopped at the front desk, probably to ask where Marion was, and the receptionist leaned to one side and started to point. Marion beat her to the punch.

"Apparently you make a habit of bullying people."

Sofia spun around. "What? I'm—"

"No, you didn't give me a chance to defend myself before you put that video on the air. So you're going to hear me now. All of the reviews you mentioned were real, I admit that, but using them means you had to dig through more than three hundred glowing reviews to find them. Anyone with reading skills above third grade could figure out that we're a good company. We care. And yes, we might screw up now and then, but those times are few and far between. You had to see that. But you chose to paint us as a no-star company that couldn't be trusted with microwaving a frozen dinner. This company is my life, and you knocked it down into the mud just because you wanted to. You had nothing to gain from it. You could have ruined everything I've worked for. What did I ever do to you?"

Sofia's mouth moved, but no words came out. "I... o-our conversation..."

"You call that a conversation? You ambushed me, just like you ambush everyone else. You're a bully. You read words off a teleprompter and edit your little videos to make us look like we're nothing. You mock the hard work we do to make ends meet. I don't know how many of the people you've taken down were legitimately bad businessmen, but I'm sure that would be an interesting report." She stepped closer, glaring into Sofia's dark eyes. "Your Back-Up segment is just an excuse to be cruel to people who are more accomplished than you'll ever be. Who have done more than you ever will. You should be ashamed of creating such a horrible, nasty thing."

Sofia's eyes had widened near the end of her speech, her lips set in a tight line. "You really ought to watch your mouth."

"Really? I'm the one who should censor myself?" She shook her head and began moving toward the door. "I'm not going to waste any more of your time. I'm sure you have a lot of other businesses to destroy with your piece of shit segment." She saluted with two fingers and turned her back on Sofia.

She was almost to the door when something smacked her in the shoulder. She looked down and saw a tissue box tumble across the floor, its side dented where it had impacted her. Her eyes widened with disbelief as she turned her gaze to Sofia. The wide-eyed stupor was gone, replaced with red cheeks and burning dark eyes. Her lips were parted to show her teeth. She looked like a wild animal that was only being held back by a frayed leash.

"I will bury you," Sofia said. "And your shitty company."

"Go to hell," Marion replied.

She tried not to hurry as she walked from the building, but she remained braced for another assault until she was completely outside with the door between her and the raging bull she'd just confronted. It felt good to fight back, to figuratively spit in the face of the woman who had said such awful things about Beacon, but common sense began crowding back in as she walked to the trolley. She couldn't help but start worrying she'd just made things infinitely worse.

The receptionist had risen to her feet when Sofia grabbed the tissue box and gasped when she actually threw it. It had taken all of her willpower not to grab something that would have really hurt, like the candy dish or the phone receiver. Her mind was filled with all the curse words, all the epithets she wanted to hurl at the bitch she'd been moments away from apologizing to. She was shaking with rage. When Marion left the building, Sofia forced her feet to remain still so she wouldn't pursue.

"Miss Kennedy?" Susie said softly. "Are you~"

"I'm fine." She tore her eyes off the empty space where Marion had just been standing and went toward the stairs.

Susie said, "Miss Kennedy, you're off today..."

"I know." She didn't trust herself to drive. She went directly to her desk, wishing she could close the door and stew in silence. Luckily she wasn't very close with the weekend morning crew so the chances were good they would just leave her alone. She rested her elbows on the desk and buried her face in her hands.

The sudden shift in her mood was enough to leave her reeling. She felt breathless and punchy. Throwing the tissue box was partially to prevent herself from doing anything worse, anything truly damaging. She felt tears stinging her eyes and angrily pressed her thumbs against the closed lids until she saw sparks. She wasn't going to cry, not at her desk, not because of Marion Vogt.

She could hear Reggie's voice in her head. They were at dinner with two of Reggie's friends, a couple who had just been kicked out of their home because of a homophobe on the condo board. They'd appealed the decision but weren't making any headway. They were resigned to losing the home they loved just because they happened to be gay.

Over drinks, Reggie casually suggested Sofia do a story on it. Sofia awkwardly tried to get out of it any way she could. "That might just make them dig their heels in further," and "It wouldn't matter in the end, because the condo board can kick people out for whatever reason they deem worthy." Their friends dropped the matter, but Reggie hadn't. She remained silent until they were getting ready for bed that night.

"Are you going to admit the real reason you won't stand up for them?"

"What?"

"Come on, Sofe. We both know why you don't want to help. It's a Gay Story." She said it so the capitalization was unmistakable. "God forbid you gain a reputation for standing up for homo rights."

Sofia got under the covers. "That's not fair. If I thought there was a chance they could be shamed into doing the right thing, of course I would present it. I'd put it down tomorrow morning. We've had laws against discrimination since the eighties. It's not a Gay Story. It's a human rights story. But there's really nothing to be done here."

Reggie's voice was gentle. "You're lying. You could make a difference. You could help our friends stay in the home they've built, but you're scared."

Sofia was glad the lights were already off. "I don't want..."

"I know." Reggie reached out and touched her in the darkness. "Baby, I know. But you have to make a decision. I'm not saying you have to come out or put yourself at risk. But you have to choose what you're willing to fight for."

The next day, Sofia suggested Back-Up to her producer. She presented it as a chance to take down unscrupulous contractors and, almost as an afterthought, mentioned discrimination cases. He liked the idea enough to give her a trial run of three segments. She spent the rest of the day digging up anything that would fit the format she'd pitched. One was a landscaper who never followed through on his promises after receiving the first check, the second was a repair shop that wasn't honoring a royalty, and the third was the condo board trying to kick out their friends. Her producer okayed all three and they set a loose schedule of when they would be aired.

A month later, the condo board reversed their decision based on "new policies" that had nothing to do with the fact they'd been profiled on the new segment. It got the attention of Lambda Legal, and members of the board were inundated with emails from outraged citizens. Their friends took them out to dinner out of gratitude, and Reggie privately thanked her for doing the right thing.

"I'm glad it worked out for both of you in the end," Reggie said. "I know your privacy is important to you. It was a choice between doing the right thing and keeping yourself safe. I honestly don't know what I would've done in your shoes."

Sofia said, "Sure you do. You wouldn't have hesitated. You would have knocked down every wall until the bad guys backed down." She rubbed Reggie's hip under the blanket. "This segment is my way of being a little bit more like you. Fighting for the people who can't fight for themselves."

Reggie smiled. "It's good to have a legacy."

And Marion Vogt had called it a piece of shit. Marion had inadvertently insulted Reggie's memory, and in return Sofia had used the segment that was supposed to be Reggie's legacy to enact petty revenge. She dropped her hands and folded them into fists in front of her face, staring at the wall ten feet in front of her desk. She needed help. She needed advice. She took out her phone and dialed Kathryn's number, chewing on her thumb until she answered. The sound of a crowd filled her ear, people shouting over a quiet murmur of casual conversation.

"Sofe?" Kathryn said over the din. "I'm at the Market! Come on down. There's a really awesome busker down here you'll love."

Sofia started to speak, but her voice broke on the first word. She hung her head, covering her eyes with her free hand.

"Sofia?"

"Can you come get me? I'm at work."

"What are you doing at... no, yeah, never mind. I'll be right there, honey."

She hung up and went to the bathroom to splash cold water on her face. When she was bent over the sink, water dripping off her face, she began crying again. Her entire relationship with Reggie, the most precious thing in her life, was a secret. She treated it like something she was ashamed of. Reggie said she understood. The entire time they were together, she accepted the fact she would never get to attend work parties or meet Sofia's friends. Sofia always thought someday, maybe in a year or two, maybe when she was established as a journalist. Maybe when she didn't have to worry about the "Lesbian Anchor" sign hanging around her neck, then she would be comfortable telling people.

Kathryn came into the bathroom. "Sofe?"

"God..." She turned away and pulled out a handful of paper towels to dry her face. "I'm fine."

"You're not fine." Kathryn put her hands on Sofia's shoulders and rubbed them. "What happened? Susie said you threw a box of tissues at someone."

Sofia said, "Yeah. Apparently I have a nemesis now."

"Cool. C'mon. I'll get you a salmon piroshky and you can tell me all about it."

Sofia turned to face Kathryn. "I'm gay."

Kathryn held her gaze. "You are?"

"Yeah."

"So... you... want a cinnamon piroshky instead...? I'm not sure what that has to do with your dessert choice..."

Sofia laughed. "Nothing. It doesn't have anything to do with that." She put her arms around her friend and hugged her. "Thank you."

"Sure, Sofe. I'd do anything for you. You know that."

Sofia sniffled and pulled back. "A salmon piroshky sounds delicious."

"Okay. Come on. We'll eat them in the car so you can spill your guts without worrying about anyone overhearing."

Sofia checked to make sure her face wasn't too puffy from crying, thankful she hadn't put on makeup that morning, and followed her friend out of the bathroom.

CHAPTER SIX

MARION PASSED by the main office window on her way into the building, so Courtney knew she was coming. Courtney came out of the office as Marion was coming through the back door, a ledger book in one hand. Courtney was the thinnest chef Marion had ever seen. The smallest size of chef coat draped her body like a shroud, and her hands stuck out of the billowing sleeves like a toy doll. But her food was the best Marion had ever tasted - her own included - so she had to assume Courtney just never tasted anything she had cooked.

She held up her hand to prevent Marion from speaking first. "I got back four of the clients who bailed after seeing the news. I had to give them pretty sweet discounts, but they're willing to give us a chance to prove ourselves."

"You're a savior," Marion said. "Thank you."

"I have the details of the discounts here."

Marion took the ledger from her. "Honestly, I'll be happy with anything under eighty percent. These numbers all look good. Courtney, thank you."

"Sure. It's my butt, too." She smiled and squeezed Marion's shoulder. "Where did you go?"

"I had a chat with Sofia Kennedy."

Courtney's eyes widened. "You did?"

"Well, more of a situation where I yelled at her and then she threw a tissue box at my head."

"What?!"

"I guess she didn't like someone standing up for themselves."

Courtney stared for another beat, then laughed. "She threw a tissue box at your head?"

Marion started laughing. "Well, technically she hit my shoulder. I don't know if that was intentional or just bad aim." She took a breath and looked around the kitchen, where her crew was busily preparing a meal for whatever event they were working that night. "Okay. I'm here, I might as well be useful. Where would I do the most good?"

"A couple of the people who cancelled asked to speak with you personally. I said you wouldn't be in until later, but..."

"I'll take care of them now. Thank you for saving my bacon this morning, Courtney."

"Stop thanking me and get on the phones."

Marion saluted and carried the ledger into the office.

They were sitting in Kathryn's car, their piroshkies eaten and their drinks mostly gone. They were watching traffic go by with Sofia's iPod providing the soundtrack. When Kathryn's straw slurped the bottom of her cup, Sofia decided they had gone long enough without speaking. She sighed, ran her hands down her thighs and looked cautiously at her best friend.

"So?"

Kathryn nodded slowly. "The piroshky was pretty good. I wish I'd gotten the salmon, though."

"No, about..."

"What?"

"The... other thing. My sexuality. I understand if you need time to process it."

Kathryn's brow wrinkled. "Process? No... I'm processed, I think. I-I'm not sure what I'm supposed to be processing."

Sofia glared at her. "The fact I'm gay."

"Uh-huh."

"Don't tell me you knew the whole time."

Kathryn said, "No. But I've known *you* the whole time. I've come to trust you. And I love you. Am I a little annoyed you made me doubt my matchmaking skills all these years when I've been using bad information? Yeah, maybe. But processing? Nothing changed about you. You've been gay the whole time I've known you."

Sofia was surprised to find her eyes watering, and she looked away to dab at them. Kathryn reached out and stroked the back of Sofia's head.

"I'm sorry. I've just spent so much time in the closet... I've never come out to anyone I care about before." She reached out and took Kathryn's hand. "Thank you for making it easy."

"Sure. I'm going to have to find a whole new hunting ground. I don't know where to pick up women seeking women."

"No," Sofia said. "No, please. Even if you found someone, I'm not ready for... I'm..." She shook her head. "I appreciate the effort, I do. But I don't want you looking."

Kathryn said, "Just because you're in the closet?"

"Among other things."

"I don't understand why you're not out. No one would care. Do you know who Nadine Butler is?" Sofia thought for a moment and then shook her head. "She's a disc jockey up near the San Juans. About ten years ago, she accidentally came out to the whole town. They tried to kick her off the air, sponsors pulled their ads from her show, there were protests... but she stood up for herself. She was promised one last show and decided she was going to see it through to the end. By the time she left the booth, the entire town had rallied behind her. She's still on the air today."

"That's a sweet story, but I don't think it would be the same for me. Besides, even if everyone was on board with it, how long would it be until I started getting assigned to all the gay-rights stories? Someone has to cover the parade, someone has to talk about discrimination, might as well shove it onto the gay anchor. I just want to be an anchor and do my job without my private life becoming my public identity. If that means I have to keep it completely secret, then that's what I have to do."

Kathryn said, "Okay. Should I keep trying to hook you up with guys?"

Sofia laughed. "Sure. Now I won't have to worry about hurting your feelings if I turn you down. You can keep all the guys for yourself."

"Oh, I've never offered you guys I was interested in. They'd be way out of your league."

Sofia laughed again and leaned across the console to hug her friend. "Thank you."

"You're welcome. Just tell me that you haven't really been alone all these years. You've dated, right? You just couldn't tell me because they were women."

"I've... had overnight guests. I haven't really dated in a long time."

"Why?"

Sofia sighed heavily. "That's a whole other kettle of worms."

Kathryn smiled. "Kettle of fish?"

"Whatever. There was someone. We adored each other."

"Reggie," Kathryn said softly. She closed her eyes and shook her head. "Reggie was a woman. Of course she was. So what happened to her?"

"She died."

Kathryn reached out and took Sofia's hand. "And you didn't think to come out to me then? Did you have anyone there to help you?"

Sofia shook her head. "I wanted to be alone."

"The sabbatical you took after..." She furrowed her brow and her gaze drifted to one side as she thought back. "Oh, god. The night you froze on-air. Please tell me that wasn't her."

"I saw her bike on the live shot."

Kathryn swore under her breath. "You should have come to me."

"I'm sorry I didn't. But I really needed to be alone. I needed to... adjust..."

She looked out the window and thought back to those dark days. She barely left her apartment, never even glanced at her phone, ignored the computer. It was easy to mourn in Seattle; the cloud cover never lifted and their balcony was constantly showered by a light, cold rain. Reggie's family dealt with the arrangements. They didn't like Sofia, didn't want to acknowledge their relationship, so she wasn't invited to the funeral. She was lucky she even knew where they laid her to rest so she could visit.

"Will you tell me about her sometime?" Kathryn asked. "I've always dreamed about you settling down with someone, having a life. Now I found out you already had it... I want to know all about her."

"I'll tell you whatever you want to know. But not right now."

Kathryn nodded. "Suddenly there's this whole side of you that I'm just finding out about. It's exciting. It's like finding out you're a superhero."

Sofia snorted. "Sleeping with women doesn't give you superpowers."

"Are you sure? How extensive has your research been?"

"Pretty extensive."

Kathryn sighed. "Whole world... hidden from your best friend. But I'll get over it."

Sofia reached out and took Kathryn's hand. "Good. So are you sure you're okay?"

"I'm fine. Are *you* okay? You were having a meltdown when you called me."

"I was... emotional. Someone said something. I don't want to get into it. Just being here with you, talking to you, is exactly what I needed."

Kathryn said, "Happy I could help. But here's what you *really* need to do. You need to go to that gym of yours and swim. Swim until you can barely stand. You need to clear your head and that's the best way to do it. Right?" Sofia nodded. "The spend the rest of the day enjoying yourself, get to bed early, and then wake up tomorrow and go for a swim before the day begins. It's like, uh, like baptism, right? Being reborn in the water, washing away everything that came before. Just wash away whatever made you snap and move on."

"That sounds really great, Kathryn. I think I'll do that."

After that they were silent again, but Sofia was willing to let it linger this time. She decided she was the one who needed to process. The person she was closest to in the world finally knew the truth. Kathryn knew about Reggie. A revelation that had seemed so monumental in the past was suddenly over and done with, and nothing had changed except that she was closer to her best friend. She knew it was just the first step in a longer journey, but she was willing to wait and enjoy that stage before moving on to the next.

That, and a nice relaxing pre-dawn swim was just what she needed to get back on track.

By noon, Marion could barely keep her eyes open. She stayed until one, when she decided that her sleep deprivation was more of a hindrance than a help. Courtney eagerly agreed to take over to Marion could go back home and get some rest. Marion started for the door, but Courtney asked her to wait while she retrieved something from her locker. Marion slumped against the wall next to the exit and closed her eyes, her adrenaline fading fast. She had never been more grateful that she couldn't afford a car and had to rely on the trolley.

"Okay," Courtney said as she approached, holding out what looked like two credit cards. One was attached to a lanyard. "Take these. I want you to sleep and relax for the rest of the day. But knowing you, you'll be climbing the walls by five o'clock tomorrow morning. I want you to take this, go to my gym, and pamper yourself. Use the sauna, take a swim. They have a fantastic pool. Work out if you want. But just promise that you'll relax."

Marion took the cards. "That sounds really phenomenal, Courtney. Thank you."

"My pleasure. The pass identifies you as my guest, and the other card will get you into the special member areas. The pool is restricted, but that early in the morning you shouldn't have too many people bugging you. But I'm serious. You had a long night and then you had a crazy morning dealing with all this nonsense. Treat yourself."

"I'll do that." She hugged Courtney. "I'm lucky to have you."

"Yes, you are. And I'm lucky you made this place what it is." She rubbed Marion's back and let her go. "I don't want to see you until tomorrow morning. After lunch, if you can restrain yourself that long."

"I'll do my best."

She said goodbye and thanked everyone else who was in the kitchen before she left. It meant the world to her that they were still toiling away even after the disastrous story, even after seeing their scheduled jobs evaporating. They had faith in Beacon, they had faith in her, and she wanted to be sure they knew it was noticed and appreciated.

When she finally pulled herself away, she had to wait almost the full ten minutes at the trolley stop until the car arrived. She was weary enough that a man wearing a hooded parka looked up and immediately offered his seat to her. She thanked him with a small smile and dropped down, sighing as she rested her shoulder against the cold condensation of the window.

She could rest easy knowing the damage done by Sofia Kennedy had been dealt with. Yes, there were a few clients who hadn't agreed to come back. Yes, there were probably other potential clients who would go with another company based on the report. But the repercussions wouldn't linger. The segment would be forgotten. Their trial was over, for the most part. She might have made a personal enemy out of the journalist, but that was a minor consideration in her mind. She'd never run into the bitch before this whole mess began and she didn't plan to start seeing her out.

Marion fished Courtney's cards from her pocket and transferred them to her purse so she wouldn't lose them. She wasn't normally a gym type of person, but a sauna and a pool sounded divine. Spending an hour swimming and then relaxing in the heat might be exactly what she needed to put Back-Up behind her once and for all. And it would be even more blissful in the morning when no one was around.

She could hardly wait until morning.

Chapter Seven

Sofia and Kathryn ended up sitting in the car for over an hour. Kathryn listened, laughed at the right spots, held Sofia's hand when the storytelling got too tough. It wasn't her intention to talk so long, but once she got going it was impossible to stop. It felt so freeing to discuss Reggie with someone. To be open and honest about her feelings for the woman she loved more than anything else in the world. When they parted, Sofia felt lighter and her mind was quieter than it had been in years. She didn't anticipate the fallout from the conversation. Sharing had opened the floodgates between memory and subconscious.

When she got home she spent the rest of the day descending deeper into depression and loneliness. She took a long bath and went to bed, hoping that a nice long sleep would her get back on track. Instead, as soon as she was out, her mind was overrun by thoughts she'd spent so long trying to keep suppressed because they hurt too much to remember.

Sofia was back in their apartment. It was dark outside the living room window, either night or her mind didn't bother filling in the exterior details.

"Why are you with me?" Sofia asked in the dream, a real question that had come up during a fight. "Honestly, what do you get out of this deal? You get a girlfriend who hides you, who acts like she's ashamed of you, someone you can't talk about or go out on a real date with. What is keeping you from walking out that door?"

And Reggie... in the dream she was dressed in a T-shirt and torn jeans, her hair sticking up in wild spikes to reveal where it had been shaved on the sides. She was barefoot and, standing next to Sofia in her heels, looked to be about half her height.

"What do I get?" Reggie responded. "I get a woman I'm crazy about. I get a woman who shuts out the whole world but lets me inside. Me and no one else. No one knows all of you the way I do, and that makes me feel special." She put her hands on Sofia's shoulders. "I love that you're taller than me, and you wear heels that make you tower over me even more. So I have to stand on my toes to kiss you and, when I do that, you put your hands on my hips and move me to the nearest flat surface. I love that Sofia Kennedy, the one on the news and on the side of the bus, is for everyone else. But I get the Sofia Kennedy who is quiet and shy, and who gets grumpy if I make her wait, or wiggles her nose when it itches instead of just scratching it like a normal person."

Sofia laughed and put her hands on Reggie's cheeks. "I got so lucky finding you."

Reggie had put her arms around Sofia's waist and stretched up to kiss her. The dream faded and spliced together with different memories. They were on the train together, not holding hands. They were eating lunch on opposite sides of the table instead of sharing a booth. After a few years of living together in secret, Sofia barely even thought about how they had to comport themselves in public. Hiding became their way of life.

They never kissed goodbye if they were in public. They never held hands. Reggie never reached out to hold Sofia's hand on the bus. For all the love and adoration shown in private, to the world they had never been more than friends. Close pals.

Sofia woke up at three in the morning unable to get back to sleep. Her chest ached, and she propped up her pillows so she could sit against the headboard. Suddenly her idea of changing her whole life to avoid memories of Reggie seemed like a horrible idea. She looked around the darkness of the bedroom and saw nothing of Reggie. No hint or memento of the woman who meant so much to her for five years.

"No," she muttered. She kicked back the blankets and turned on a lamp, dropping to her knees to yank open the bottom drawer of the nightstand. She had to have saved something. There must have been a T-shirt or a book. Some little piece of the love of her life that had escaped the purge. She left the drawer open and rushed down the hallway. Why had she scrubbed her life clean? How could unexpected reminders hurt worse than complete erasure?

She searched the living room, tossing aside her shoes and sunglasses and her raincoat. The lamps were new. The clock hanging on the partition between the living room and kitchen was new. She was trembling as she stood and turned in a slow circle around the home she now barely recognized. Where were Reggie's shoes? Where was the poster-sized painting of a wet Audrey Hepburn laughing in a pool that had once hung so prominently next to the closet door?

She remembered throwing out the shoes. The poster had been gifted to their friends Nate and Charlie who always coveted it. And now she had nothing.

Before she completely gave in to despair, she remembered their videos. She went to the closet, retrieved the laptop case from the top shelf, and carried it into the living room. It hadn't been turned on in years, so she also brought the power cord and plugged it in. It was Reggie's laptop and should've been tossed with everything else, but some part of her had apparently anticipated this breakdown. She told herself there were a lot of necessary files saved on it, that it was too expensive to just toss out, that she had no particular attachment to a piece of technology that Reggie had barely ever used anyway.

She waited for it to boot up and then opened the folder marked labeled "For You." She clicked on one at random and the window opened. Her eyes were already watering when the video started playing. It started with a sweeping shot of the water before the phone was turned around to show Reggie's face. Sofia gasped out a sob and put a hand over her mouth, admitting now that these videos were the reason she saved the laptop.

"This is for you," she said, "since you can't be here right now. I'm on the ferry coming in from Bainbridge. I had a really good day this morning. Lots of work stuff, wheels put in motion. Looks like you might not be the only one bringing in money soon." She held up a hand with her fingers crossed and winked before turning the camera around again. "So just imagine you're standing here next to me, telling me it's going to work out, and I'm going to pretend I'm holding your hand instead of this phone. It's gorgeous out here. Cold, though. If you want the full experience, I'm going to have to ask you to stick your head in the freezer while you're watching this."

Sofia laughed and wiped her palm across her cheek. They both filmed "For You" videos, little snippets of life and commuting that they couldn't share in person for fear of someone seeing them. Reggie once said it was like other couples who had phone sex. "We can't be affectionate in public, so we do it over the phone. We save the sexiness for behind closed doors." The videos ranged from a few minutes to half an hour. Sofia watched them at random, laughing at the funny ones and blinking away tears at the ones where Reggie just aimed the camera at her face as she walked through downtown.

She watched for an hour until her emotional mood swings became too much. She turned off the computer but left it plugged in so she could watch more when she got home. She threw on a pair of sweats and used a cap and glasses to disguise herself. She wasn't in the mood for a round of "Hey, aren't you...?" with the people of Seattle. She needed the pool. She needed to be submerged.

The gym was deserted save for a girl at the front desk and a few paunchy, balding types in the main workout room. Sofia passed them and went directly to the elevator, swiping her key and stepping into the car. She sighed and closed her eyes, impatiently willing time to move faster so she could be in the water. Reggie laughed about her addiction, but it was the truth. She was utterly addicted to swimming. The freedom to escape gravity, to shut out the noise, to use muscles to propel her through the world... it was like flying.

When she arrived at the pool, she took a moment to absorb the atmosphere of what was, to her, a sacred place. It was several degrees cooler than the rest of the building due to all the glass and tile. She could hear the water lapping against the edges of the pool as she went to the locker room and changed into her swimsuit. It was a navy blue one-piece, Reggie's favorite color, and she smoothed her hands over her stomach before retrieving her towel.

The door between the pool and the main hall had a glass window at eye level. Through it she could see someone was already inside, a woman standing at the edge of the pool with her back to the door. She was wearing a black swimsuit that was cut low to reveal her back. The Lycra hugged the curves of her ass and Sofia paused to appreciate the view. The other woman brought both arms over her head and stretched lazily, tilting to one side and then the other.

Sofia could seduce her. It wasn't a "Reggie Day," and having sex could go a long way to clearing up any remaining cobwebs in her mind. Sofia wasn't superficial or picky about her lovers, but this woman at least had a great body. They could race each other, then one of them would cross the lane. She bit her bottom lip as she imagined the water lapping against their bodies as she pushed aside the crotch of the stranger's suit. They wouldn't even know each other's names.

She finally decided to stop ogling and pushed open the door, the sound of the push bar echoing through the room. The other woman had been poised to dive, but she turned at the sound of the new arrival. Sofia glanced at her, curious to see if her face matched the rest of her body, and slowed in her tracks. She knew she must have been overtired or remembering wrong, but the other woman's eyes widened and her shoulders fell.

"You've got to be kidding me," Marion Vogt said.

Sofia said, "This is a members' only area. You can't be here."

"I have a guest pass. My friend thought I needed to unwind after everything you've done to me this week. You know, torpedoing my work, throwing a Kleenex box at me. What are *you* doing here? Unwinding after a long day of attacking another small business owner?"

"This is my pool. This is my time of day. I'm not going to let you spoil that. The pool is big enough for the both of us."

"Fine."

Sofia gave Marion a wide berth, tossed her towel onto the rack, and suppressed a sigh as she walked to the pool's edge. Marion dived and broke the water with a surprisingly minimal splash before she transitioned into a smooth breaststroke. She used a frog kick, pushing herself forward quickly as her arms cut through the water. Sofia watched as she stretched and then dived as well. She put on more speed than she ordinarily would have in a first lap, taking note of where Marion was every time she turned her head. Marion reached the wall first and executed a flawless turn, already on her way back to the starting point when Sofia slapped the wall.

Marion seemed to be moving faster on the return trip, and Sofia understood that it really was a race. She sacrificed style for speed, ignoring her competitor except when she made her turns. At the end of the first lap she was only a few seconds behind Marion. By the second, they were neck and neck. Their hands slapping against the side of the pool happened in such quick succession that the echo made it almost impossible to tell which one hit first.

They swam laps for nearly half an hour. Occasionally one would overtake the other, but neither was able to take a commanding lead. The competition came to an abrupt halt when Marion reached the wall a few seconds before Sofia and, instead of turning once more, came to a complete stop. She rested her arms on the edge of the pool and looked toward Sofia's lane, her legs drifting out behind her. Sofia knew that if she stopped, she would be acknowledging it had been a race. She hadn't been paying close enough attention to be certain of victory, so she turned and did one more lap for good measure. If she hadn't beaten Marion in time, she had certainly gotten the better distance.

By the time she ended her lap, Marion was toweling off and going back to the locker room. Sofia stopped and relaxed, her shoulders aching from pushing herself so hard without the proper warm-up. She thought about just floating for a bit so she wouldn't run into Marion in the locker room, but she didn't want to seem afraid. She'd had fantasies like this. A silent competition in an empty pool, then crossing paths in the locker room. "I haven't had a swim like that in years," she would have said. "We should do that more often." A touch that might have been innocent, a lingering glance before going to the showers, and then...

She growled at herself and splashed water up into her face. She really needed to get laid.

When her muscles were relaxed, she pushed herself up out of the pool and wrapped the towel around herself. Marion was at a locker that Sofia had to pass to get to her own, because of course she was. Sofia made a show of drying her hair with the towel so avoiding eye contact wouldn't seem so rude. Marion had been looking at her phone but she quickly shut off the screen as Sofia walked behind her. It was a quick move, but not quick enough; Sofia recognized the messages page of the MEOW website from her brief time using the app. She had matched with a few intriguing ladies, but far too many of them recognized her from the news. She covered by saying she was doing a story on various dating apps and quickly retreated from the interaction.

Marion vanished from the locker room while Sofia was showering, so she dressed quickly to make her escape as fast as possible. She regretted not getting time in the sauna, but with the luck she was having the catering bitch would be there. She would just complete her routine another day. She smiled perfunctorily at the desk clerk and headed outside, slowing as the automatic doors slid open to reveal Marion lurking outside, leaning against the wall, looking down at her phone.

"Oh, that's very mature," Sofia said.

Marion looked up at her. "What..."

"Waiting out here for me? What is this, high school? Are you going to rough me up and steal my lunch money now?"

"You're the only one here who has assaulted anybody," Marion said.

Sofia moved forward. "I had my reasons."

"What possible vendetta could you have against me? I've never met you before the other day. I'm completely confused why you decided I'm public enemy number one because of a single poor review, something I'm still not convinced had anything to do with my business."

"You don't think," Sofia said, "you just say whatever comes into your head no matter how it might affect anyone else."

Marion said, "Is this because I said you were bad at your job? You said the exact same thing to me and put it on television. If either of us has the right to be mad, it's me. If either of us has the right to want revenge, it's *me*. But I want to just let this go and move on."

"Then why are you waiting for me out here?"

A car had pulled up at the curb during their conversation, but Sofia had ignored it until she heard the driver's side door open. "Uber for Marion?" the man said.

Marion's lips curled up in the barest hint of a smile, her eyes locked on Sofia. "I'm Marion. Sorry. We were just having a little disagreement." She brushed by Sofia, bumping her shoulder as she passed. "Whatever feud we're having is entirely in your head, Miss Kennedy. You want it to end? Leave me the hell alone."

As she got into the car, the driver aimed a finger at Sofia. "Hey. I know you..."

"No, you don't," Sofia muttered, walking toward her car as quickly as she could without running. "Nobody does."

CHAPTER EIGHT

MARION STEWED over the encounter all the way home, ignoring the Uber driver's attempts to talk. Was she doomed to constant run-ins with Sofia Kennedy for the rest of her life? Would the glowering, grumpy brunette be everywhere she turned? Under any other circumstances she might have called it fate and considered herself lucky. Sofia Kennedy wasn't just TV gorgeous, she was even beautiful in sweats at five in the morning. She pushed thoughts of her apparent rival out of her mind and stared out the window for the remainder of the ride. The sun was just starting to break between the buildings of downtown and the streets were filling with people on their way to work.

The driver dropped her off in front of her apartment just as her phone rang. She saw Courtney's name on the screen and closed her eyes, whispered, "Please, good news," and answered. "Please, good news," she repeated with her full voice.

"I know what caused people to get sick at the party."

Marion paused at the door. "Was it our fault?"

Courtney said, "Oh. I didn't think you would phrase it that way. Technically, I suppose so."

"No. God..."

"Wait. We're not liable at all. People were made sick because of something we provided, but it's not our fault they got sick. God, this fell apart fast. That's what I get for being cute."

Marion said, "Just lay it out for me. Please."

"The party started at five o'clock. Samuel Flynn's schedule was that the party would begin with a toast and then food would be served an hour later, around dinner time. We served champagne during that hour to a bunch of people who hadn't eaten since lunchtime, which at that office is usually around eleven am. Add to that number anyone who worked through lunch and hadn't eaten since breakfast, and you have a dozen or so people who were chugging champagne on empty stomachs."

Marion said, "Which would lead to them getting drunk faster."

"And upset their stomachs. People must have been throwing up, doubled over, and going home early claiming they 'didn't feel well' because they didn't want to admit to their boss that they were drunk. He jumped to the reasonable conclusion and assumed we were to blame. Flynn was looking at the big picture, but when I asked the individuals who said they became sick, it got clear really fast what happened. I'm going to call Flynn and see if I can smooth things out, but I thought you should hear it first."

Marion let herself relax. "Courtney, you are going to get the biggest raise I can think of. Thank you so much for handling this."

"Nah, I owe you. I've been sneaking cupcakes from job sites. Thousands of dollars' worth of cupcakes, snuck under the table."

Marion laughed. "I'm still the boss. I can give you a raise if I want to."

"Are you coming in today? We have the wedding at four."

"I am." She checked the time on her phone. "I didn't get a chance to shower at the gym, so I'll do that and then head in."

"Oh! You went to the gym. How was the pool? Spectacular, right?"

Marion decided she couldn't fault the gym for its lax membership standards. "It was amazing. I may have to get a membership there myself."

"We could be workout buddies. I have to go. I'm getting another call."

"Hold down the fort."

"Always."

Marion hung up and leaned against the wall, breathing in the crisp morning air and truly appreciating it. The possibility, minor though it might have been, that she was responsible for people getting sick had been hanging over her like a shroud. Now she could breathe again, she could see clearly, she could relax. She looked down at her phone and drummed her fingers on the back of the case. Thinking clearly meant acting maturely, meant doing the big thing. She went upstairs so she could make the call from the comfort of her home turf.

The station's number was easy enough to find. She dialed the main reception desk and briefly wondered if she'd be speaking to someone who witnessed the tissue box assault.

"KCTV, how can we help you today?"

"Hi. This is Marion Vogt. I was wondering if I could..." She scratched her eyebrow, unsure what she needed. "Ah, if I could speak to someone involved with the Back-Up segment... on the news..."

"Oh..."

Marion heard a whole mountain of misgivings in that syllable. "No, I'm not going to jump down anyone's throat or issue a complaint or anything like that. We've conducted our own investigation into the incident and we think we know why people were getting sick. We just want a chance to defend ourselves."

The receptionist hesitated. "Okay. Well, Miss Kennedy isn't available at the moment, but I can connect you to her producer."

"Sure," Marion said.

"Hold please."

A few seconds later, the producer answered. Marion went through her reason for calling again. When she finished, he said, "We're definitely interested in showing your side of the argument, Miss Vogt, and follow-ups are always a good thing. It shows that the segment produces results."

Marion rolled her eyes.

"If you're willing, we could do a phone interview with you and have Sofia record the questions at a later date."

Marion was already imagining a horrible scenario where Sofia recorded horribly out of context questions that would make the pre-recorded answers sound callous or angry, but all she had to do was keep her cool and stick to the facts. "That would be fine. I'd like my assistant manager to be involved in the call as well. She was truly instrumental in solving this problem. Can we arrange the call for this afternoon? Say two o'clock?"

"Sounds perfect."

She gave him a number where he could call her back, then texted Courtney that they would be having a conversation with him together. Courtney sent back a thumbs-up. Marion stood and carried her phone to the window. She opened the MEOW app and went back to the message that had distracted her at the gym. Messages on the app were called "Purrs," something she could never quite bring herself to say out loud. It was just a bit too cutesy. The Purr was from a restaurant manager in Bothell named Penny. She'd seen the segment and recognized Marion's picture from the story.

"We went through something similar a few years ago. Sometimes you can do everything right and something will still go wrong. Don't let it get you down. Learn from it. If the problem was on your end, fix whatever the problem was and do better in the future. Your business will be better for this trial. Trust me. Mine was."

Marion smiled as she re-read the message. After hesitating for a long moment, she sent a reply. "That means a lot. Thank you. It looks like things will be working out, so right now the only thing I have to worry about is the fact I missed those damned emails. I appreciate you reaching out with the pep talk." She chewed her bottom lip and looked outside. "Would you want to get a drink sometime? I could head up to Bothell or you could come down here."

It wasn't too forward. It was a dating app. People expected to get hit on, right? She rolled her eyes at herself and put the phone down before she sent a message retracting the offer. She showered and got dressed for work. When she came back, there was a new Purr waiting.

"I'll be downtown Tuesday night at a bar called Thigh High. 9oclock?"

Marion chewed her bottom lip. It sounded an awful lot like a date. It was probably a date. Did she want a date? She kept her thumbs poised over the keyboard before she finally replied.

"That sounds good. I can find Thigh High. See you there."

She twisted her lips, unsure if she'd made a good decision. In the end it didn't really matter; if it was bad, at worst she would get a nice night out. She put her phone in her bag, checked to make sure she had everything she needed, and headed to work.

Sofia spent Sunday watching "For You" videos. The joy she got from hearing her lover's voice again, from seeing her smile and the way she enjoyed life faded as soon as she put the laptop away. She was left feeling maudlin and too depressed to do anything other than drink and listen to music. She read an email from her producer saying they had a follow-up interview with Marion Vogt that helped clear up the issue with Flynn's complaint. He wanted her to record the other side of the interview to air in Monday night's newscast. She grimaced and put off replying until she was in a better mood.

She sat on the futon near the window and looked toward downtown. At some point she drifted off and the combination of alcohol and binge-watching the videos filled her brain with memories of Reggie.

She pictured their lazy Sundays together. Reggie in shorts and a cable-knit sweater, lounging on the sofa with a book or the newspaper.

"Why are you wearing a sweater?"

"I'm cold."

"If you're cold, put on some pants."

"Are you complaining about seeing my legs?"

"No... that has nothing to do with it. I just don't see the point of your outfit."

"It's comfortable."

"But cold."

"Mm-hmm."

She smiled in her sleep, her head against the window. Reggie in the rain, the hood of her slicker up with rivulets spilling off the peak in front of her face. Reggie in one of her dark moods. In between work, depressed, grumpy and quiet. She called those moments Reggie's rages as a joke. Reggie never raised her voice or threw tantrums when she was sad. She just got quiet and introverted and brooded around the apartment until the mood lifted. Reggie on the couch on mornings when she didn't have to work, a big kid in her pajamas and searching the cable networks for cartoons.

Sofia's dream drifted to a breakfast scene that could have been any number of mornings in their relationship. Reggie, her robe hanging around her stool like a private eye's trench coat, hunched over her plate of pancakes and scrambled eggs, and Sofia sitting across the counter from her with a cup of coffee and her smartphone.

"You're being ridiculous," Reggie said. "The lady obviously didn't know what she was saying or how much it would hurt you. Why are you so determined to make her pay for one mistake?"

"Two mistakes," Sofia responded without looking up.

"You're not a vindictive person, Sofe. You're not petty. So stop punishing this woman for a crime she doesn't even realize she committed. Be the bigger person. Let the matter drop."

Sofia sighed and opened her eyes. There was a moment of panic as she looked down at the street before she remembered her head was against the glass. She sat up and rubbed her eyes. She didn't believe in ghosts or messages from beyond, but she knew when her own common sense was trying to nudge her in the right direction. She hadn't been listening to the still and quiet voice on its own, so it decided to use Reggie's voice to drive the point home.

She could just imagine Reggie's twisting lips, the sardonic smile as she listened to Sofia laying out what had happened. "So, what, you're going to war because this lady accidentally besmirched my honor? Babe, there's chivalry and then there's just nuts. Settle down, Sofe."

"You're right," she whispered. She looked at the empty beer bottle and pushed up out of the chair. She walked into the kitchen to put the bottle into recycling. She picked up her phone and opened the email. Reggie would have told her it was time to end things. She would have thanked Sofia for standing up for her, but it had gone on long enough.

Sofia sent back a reply saying she would put together the follow-up as soon as she got into work on Monday. With any luck, it would be the end of her interaction with Marion Vogt and Beacon Craft & Catering Service. She turned off her phone so she wouldn't be distracted by any further attempts at communication with the outside world. If she went to bed right away, there was a chance she could slip back into dreams populated by Reggie.

CHAPTER NINE

THE BEST part to the resolution of what Marion was calling "the Back-Up Fiasco" was that it didn't require her to speak with Sofia Kennedy again. She and Courtney talked with a producer over the phone, and then their comments were seamlessly edited into a segment that aired Monday at eleven. They watched together to make sure the reporter didn't skew it into some other bizarre angle, but she seemed remarkably professional throughout.

"Looks like the fire died down a little," Courtney said. "She almost came off as unbiased."

"Thank goodness for small favors," Marion said.

By Wednesday, the entire ordeal was basically forgotten. They had some holes in their events schedule, but they were getting new clients every day. Weddings and mitzvahs and more concerts needed food and weren't swayed by the damning segment. In less than a week they were going at full steam once more. Marion allowed herself a bit of relief at how quickly they'd gotten everything back on the rails. Courtney's raise was an immediate change on the payroll. She had jumped to action to make sure the damage was minimal, so she deserved to enjoy the reward just as immediately.

With things back to normal, she allowed herself to relax and take half the day off to prepare for her meeting with Penny from Bothell. She'd only met with a handful of women off the MEOW app, with varying degrees of success. Usually they just got drinks, only once or twice had they actually sat down to a full meal. She'd had sex with two of them. Nothing fantastic, but serviceable for both parties. She didn't even know if the meet-up with Penny was an official date or not. At the moment just meeting with someone new sounded like just what the doctor ordered.

Thigh High was a tiny little club near the University. Its location made her dread a crowd of goonish frat boys and perky college girls, but she arrived to find the bar was on a quiet street and seemed to cater more to professors and faculty than the students. Subdued without coming off as dull, she took a seat at the bar and ordered a drink. It arrived at the same time someone put a hand on her shoulder.

"Marion?"

She turned and smiled. "Penny? Hi."

Penny looked better than her profile picture but, to be fair, Marion had never met anyone who looked worse. Pictures were posed or weirdly angled and could never quite match the reality of someone's face. The difference for Penny, however, was larger than most. Gorgeous blue eyes, long shining black hair, and cheekbones that could cut glass. Her mouth was wide and her lips thin, and when she smiled she looked like the Cheshire cat preparing a rhyme. Marion waited for Penny to get a drink and suggested they move to a table in the corner. A small dance area was set up around the jukebox, and two middle-aged couples were taking advantage of the Aimee Mann song that was currently playing.

"Thanks for coming," Marion said. "I wanted to thank you for the pep talk. This weekend I felt like the whole world was conspiring against me. So a few kind words went a long way."

"I just remembered what it was like when I was going through it. I had friends and coworkers to lean on, but it would've meant a lot to know I didn't have to worry about the entire world hating me." Her smile widened and she dipped her head shyly. "And... it was a good opening line. I recognized you on the app from seeing you on the news. I thought you were really attractive, so I couldn't pass up the chance to reach out."

"I'm glad you did. I haven't been out in ages. I needed a chance to unwind."

"I'm glad, too. I didn't need to unwind, but... I just wanted a chance to hang out with someone attractive."

Marion took a sip to cover her smile. She didn't take

compliments well, especially when they came from beautiful women. She glanced toward the jukebox as the song ended. Both couples were returning to their seats, leaving the floor empty.

"Would you like to dance?"

She wasn't sure where the question came from. She wasn't a dancer. She could fake her way through a bit of swaying, but mostly it was just an exercise in waiting until the music stopped and she could sit down again. But for some reason she was very glad when Penny nodded, took another sip, and pushed back her seat. The Aimee Mann song had ended and the next hadn't started playing, so Marion went to the jukebox to select something for them to dance to. She inserted a dollar and chose a Norah Jones song called "Heart of Mine," which was slow enough to dance to but not overly suggestive. She joined Penny on the floor and they awkwardly both moved to take the lead. They both began to adjust, but Penny shook her head.

"I can bear following for one song."

"Are you sure?"

"Yeah," Penny chuckled and let Marion lead. "That doesn't bode well for our compatibility, does it?"

"People have made it work with bigger issues."

Penny nodded. "Yeah."

Marion said, "So do you meet up with a lot of people you meet on the app?"

"Not many. Probably the same amount of people I meet at bars. I just don't like the whole idea of selling yourself in a paragraph. You get a profile full of all the perks, all the good stuff."

"The highlights," Marion said. "By the time you see the dark parts, or the things that might be deal-breakers, you're already invested. So you tell yourself it isn't so bad, you can learn to live with it, or maybe you can change them..."

Penny said, "Exactly."

"So you like knowing the bad stuff."

"I do. They're necessary to the whole picture. If you can get the bad stuff out of the way first, then the good stuff mashes it down a little more. Makes it a bit more tolerable."

Marion said, "Makes sense. So we can be completely honest with each other."

"Right. Like we could have sat here forcing conversation for an hour, when all I'm really hoping for is a quick orgasm in the backseat of my car."

Marion lifted an eyebrow and pursed her lips. "Hm. I mean, I'm not against conversation. But I think the odds are against us being a good couple. I mean, you're all the way up in Bothell. That's, what, a half-hour drive?"

"Oof. On a good day, maybe."

"Probably not worth the effort."

"I concur."

"And I'm not against the idea of a quick orgasm in the backseat, if you're planning to reciprocate."

"Oh, absolutely. It would be rude not to."

Marion smiled and bit her bottom lip. They waited until the song ended before leaving the bar. Penny had parked at the far end of the lot, near a wall of foliage that would help block them from the street. Her spot was at the very edge of the streetlight's glow, in its reach but not as if they were onstage. She unlocked the car and slid into the backseat and, after a glance around to make sure they weren't being observed, Marion followed.

"So do you do this a lot with women on MEOW?" Marion asked as she pulled the door shut behind her.

"Only the ones I find insanely attractive."

"Good answer."

Penny slid her hand along Marion's shoulder to the back of her neck, under the blonde hair, and pulled her closer. When they kissed, Marion put her hand on the outside of Penny's thigh. She brushed her palm upward, teasing with her fingertips until she reached the edge of her skirt. Penny sank back onto the seat, pulling Marion on top of her, and they found a comfortable position with Marion positioned between Penny's legs. One knee was pinned between Marion's side and the back of the seat.

"It's not digging into you, is it?"

"No, no. It's fine," Marion said.

"Good."

Their lips met again and Penny moved her hand up into Marion's hair. Marion's hand continued its trek as well, forcing Penny to adjust her hips and pull her skirt up. Penny nipped at Marion's bottom lip, pulling it just enough for a sting but not enough to actually hurt. Marion still made a sound of surprise.

"Sorry," Penny whispered. "I can get a bit wild. One of those downsides I mentioned..."

"Who said it was a downside? Wild can be a plus?"

Penny grinned and snapped her teeth before craning her neck

up to continue their kiss. Marion got her hand between Penny's thighs. She was wearing underwear, a disappointing barrier that meant at least their current entanglement wasn't entirely planned. Marion twisted the cotton out of the way and rubbed her fingers against Penny's outer lips, gathering the moisture there before she ventured further. Penny moaned into her mouth before twisting to kiss Marion's jaw and then down her neck. One hand was still gripping the back of Marion's neck, but the other had journeyed along Marion's back to her ass, massaging it through her slacks.

"You seemed like a jeans girl on your profile..."

"I wanted to dress up for you," Marion said, more than a little breathless.

Penny said, "Mm, I'm flattered. Besides, this feels so much better." She squeezed one cheek of Marion's ass, then swatted her. "Is that okay?"

"Yeah," Marion said.

Penny moved her hand in a wide circle over Marion's ass, squeezing it a few times before she spanked her again. Marion shifted her weight forward and began to thrust, grunting as she eased her middle finger into Penny. They both gasped, and Marion lifted her head to give the windows a cursory glance. She had a vision of getting caught, of making the news, of Sofia Kennedy sharing the news that her enemy had been caught fucking a gorgeous Amazon in the parking lot of a neighborhood bar. She smiled at the mental image.

Eat your heart out, Sofia Kennedy, Marion thought as she sat up, pulling out of Penny's arms. Penny remained on her back.

"Undress me," Marion said.

"So demanding."

"Well, I let you lead on the dance floor," Marion said.

Penny's teeth flashed in the dim light as she brought her hands to the top button on Marion's blouse. Soon the material hung open to expose her chest and the cream-and-lavender bra. Penny spread her fingers over the newly-exposed territory, cupped the breasts, scraped her nails down Marion's stomach. Her eyes rolled back as Marion added a second finger and pressed her thumb against Penny's clit. She grunted low in her throat and arched up off the seat.

"Coming..." Penny grunted, unnecessarily announcing what was crystal clear even in the darkness. Her shoulders hitched, her mouth dropped open, and she curled her fingers in the waistband of

Marion's slacks like she was gripping the bridle of a bucking bronco. Marion watched her; one of her favorite things was to watch a woman in the grips of a powerful orgasm, and the sight was almost enough to get her off as well. Almost.

When Penny was still again, breathing hard and heavy-eyed, Marion bent down and kissed her, slipping her tongue into Penny's mouth and retreating when she tried to meet it.

"I want you to go down on me," Marion whispered.

"Yeah," Penny said, voice trembling, nodding eagerly as Marion sat up. Penny pulled her legs to her chest and repositioned herself on the driver's side of the car as Marion awkwardly removed her pants. Her underwear went with it, and she wadded them together and dumped them into the passenger seat to get them out of her way. She turned and put her back against the door, lifting her leg as Penny bent down to stretch out across the seat.

Marion gasped as Penny dragged her tongue up the inside of her thigh, pausing to nip and suck before moving closer to her goal. Marion put one hand in Penny's hair and braced the other against the back of the seat. Her lower body jerked when Penny kissed her labia, her toes curling at each kiss and swipe of the tongue that followed. She slid lower, lifting her hips as Penny slid one hand underneath to cup her ass. Penny's tongue was long and flat, and she put it to remarkable use.

Marion rolled her head back and looked out the window over the top of her head. She saw the streetlight high above her, the shapes distorted by the glass, and she smiled.

"Wild thing," she muttered, and Penny's answering laugh caused delicious vibrations to wash through her. She bit her bottom lip and put both hands on the back of Penny's head to guide her through the sure-to-be-too-brief remainder of their time together.

Afterward, they helped each other dress. Penny retrieved Marion's pants from the front seat ("Your panties nearly ended up on the dashboard. Might have been an interesting sight to anyone walking by.") and they kissed for a few minutes just to assure the other their time together hadn't been solely about the physical release. They exchanged numbers and email addresses before Penny offered to drive Marion home so she wouldn't have to wait for the trolley. Marion agreed, though she was aware of the dangers of showing a relative stranger where she lived.

"You're not a stalker, ax-murderer, insane type, are you?"

Penny laughed. "No. I swear. At worst, I may call you up for another round if I'm still single in a month. But next time we'll have to find a bed."

"I have a bed."

"Oh!"

"And it should be much easier for you to get a nice clearance..." She mimed swatting.

Penny laughed. "Yeah. That's, um... that's usually a fourth date sort of thing."

"I'm glad you skipped ahead. I have a few things I usually save for the fourth date, too. I might have to bring them out if you call me again."

"Can't wait."

She parked at the curb outside Marion's building. "It's a real bummer that things won't work out for us."

"It is. But we're both way too dominant. It's fun every now and then..."

"But we'd be tearing each other apart inside a month."

"But hey, angry sex!"

Penny laughed and stroked Marion's cheek with the back of one finger. "I'm glad we met each other."

"Me too." She leaned in and kissed Penny goodbye, climbed out of the car, and watched her until the taillights disappeared around the corner. She sighed, rolled her shoulders, and went inside. A relationship was a lot of work, and she really needed to focus on getting Beacon back on track. Things were going well. She didn't want to risk being distracted with romantic entanglements.

But a few no-strings-attached romps with a gorgeous woman? That was definitely something she could work into her schedule.

Chapter Ten

Four Months Later

"...AND WE'RE back in four, three." The producer finished counting down on his fingers. Sofia looked up from her copy as the cameras moved in on the news desk. She smiled and affected an amused tone for the lightweight story they always ended broadcasts with. It was some fluff designed to put the audience at ease enough to sleep after all the horrible news stories they had been subjected to over the past half hour.

"We're going to leave you tonight with this video that's been making the rounds on Facebook and all the social media today. A few years back we showed you a dog that had learned to take the bus to the park by itself. Well, that dog may have finally met his match. This is Daisy, and Daisy's owner says that she was shocked one morning last week when he answered the door and discovered that Daisy had used his phone to order a pizza."

They played the short clip of the Ballard man explaining how the collie had apparently manipulated his smartphone onto the proper website and sent off an order. Sofia spent the fifteen seconds with her eyes on the clock. Evan and Reed joined her and Del at the main desk for the last shot. Sofia ignored them and smiled into the lens they came back to the live shot.

"Just goes to show you should always lock your phones when

you're not using them," she said, turning to face Del.

"Could've been worse," Del said. "Could've had the phone on Amazon. He might have ended up with a new car."

Sofia laughed even though her natural response was to say Amazon didn't sell vehicles. She gathered her papers and stacked them, a signal of finality that meant the news was over.

"Thank you for joining us tonight, and we hope you have a wonderful night."

Del said the line about staying tuned for the late-night talk show that followed the broadcast, some grinning white male buffoon interviewing other rich white male buffoons about whatever they were up to that particular week. Sofia hated promoting such nonsense, so she let Del take it. The music swelled as the lights dimmed. Del turned to Evan and began talking about the dog in the video as she pretended to make notes on her copy of the script. She drew a circle around one block of dialogue, then added petals so it would become a flower.

"Good show tonight," Reed said.

"You too."

"Do you have plans for the weekend? I was thinking maybe we could meet up somewhere~"

Sofia said, "Plans. Sorry. I'm meeting a friend who is coming in from Lawrence, Kansas. I haven't seen her for ages."

Reed nodded. "Okay. Just thought I'd make the offer."

She smiled politely and pushed her chair back. She wanted to make her escape as hasty as possible. She didn't like small-talk with her fellow anchors who focused on sports she didn't watch or weekend plans she never intended to join them on. Then there was Reed, who had been trying to get into her pants from the day they started working together.

Reggie had always laughed when she complained. "You know, sweetheart, you could just surrender."

"Sleep with Reed?"

"Ugh, no," Reggie dispelled the idea with a wave of her hands. "No, I meant just come out to them already. They love you. The audience loves you. Public opinion is one hundred percent on the side of anti-discrimination. If the producers are idiotic enough to fire you just because you come out, they'd have a legal battle on their hands."

Sofia said, "And they're smart enough to know that. They wouldn't fire me outright. They would start moving me around to 'special coverage.' They'd promote someone like Kathryn or Steve to my place at the desk while pretending my new assignments were a promotion. I'd go from five nights a week to one segment every couple of days. They'd make me invisible."

"You're already invisible," Reggie said. "You made yourself invisible by hiding who you are."

"There's only one person I want to know who I am." Sofia reached out and took Reggie's hand. "You know me. That's enough."

Reggie smiled. She was sitting with her foot up on the couch, and she rested her chin on the bent knee. "But I want to share you."

"Be careful," Sofia said. "If I'm spread too thin, I might disappear for real."

She sat down at her desk and found a handful of phone messages waiting. One of them was a mechanic returning her call about a new Back-Up segment, so she moved that to the top of the pile. She would call them back in the morning and hopefully arrange a meeting where she could confront the owner about the complaints he'd gotten. She glanced up at movement near the entrance of the newsroom and sat up straighter when she saw it was Kathryn.

"Hey. I thought you'd gone home ages ago."

"I did. I came back. What are you doing tomorrow?"

Sofia bristled and considered pulling out her lie about Lawrence, Kansas, again. "I'm sure I'll think of something as soon as the other shoe drops."

Kathryn rolled her eyes. "There's a party on Whidbey Island. A bunch of artsy-types, a few actors, some local celebrities. But here's the thing: discretion is the name of the game. A bunch of people who will be there are closeted–"

"I just thought of something I have to do tomorrow night."

"Come on, Sofe."

She gathered her things and lowered her voice. "The very fact you're bringing this up at work..."

"No one is here," Kathryn said, sweeping her arm to indicate the empty room. Half the fluorescent lights had been turned off to save energy, casting deep shadows all around them.

"It doesn't matter, Kathryn. It doesn't matter if you think you're being careful or sneaky. I don't want to go to some party no matter how discreet it's supposed to be. You're playing fast and loose with a secret that isn't yours to share." She walked to the exit, aware that

Kathryn was hurrying to catch up with her but not particularly caring.

Kathryn intercepted her in the lobby and hooked an arm around her elbow so she wouldn't escape. Sofia rolled her eyes and continued walking outside, to her car, where Kathryn finally let her go to walk around to the passenger side.

"Am I driving you home?"

"You want private? The car is private."

Sofia got behind the wheel and Kathryn got into the passenger seat. Kathryn put her bag in her lap. Kathryn spoke first. "I'm sorry. You're right. I'm being sloppy and risking the privacy you so obviously cherish. I apologize for that. But I still think you should go to this party. Everyone there will be someone like you. Someone who thinks letting themselves be open with the world is career suicide. You won't have to worry about anyone recognizing you or leaking your secret."

"I could get the same thing just by staying at home."

"Aren't you sick of that place yet? Aren't you sick of being alone?"

Sofia looked down at her hands. "I'm not ready to put someone else in the empty space."

Kathryn reached over and squeezed Sofia's shoulder. "I wish I'd known Reggie so I could tell you she didn't want this. She wouldn't want you going through a routine, going through the motions of life. Would she have let you hunker down in your apartment for weeks on end, never going out, never enjoying this beautiful city?"

Sofia sighed. "It hurts to go out. To see things I'll never be able to tell Reggie about."

"I know, honey. But you need to keep going."

"Damn it," Sofia muttered. "Where is this damn party?"

Kathryn grinned and took out her phone. "It's in Oak Harbor on Whidbey Island. I swear, Sofe, you're going to have a great time. It isn't about hooking up or meeting people, it's just about socializing without hiding. We're talking about a group of intelligent, charming people who are finally getting a chance to be themselves."

"And it's... I mean, how do you know the secrecy is enforced?"

"Because of the non-disclosure agreements. Everyone who goes to the party signs an agreement that they won't blab. The host is a guy who has held this sort of get-together before and it's always gone well. No one has ever been outed after one of them."

Sofia narrowed her eyes. "You'd tell me if this was an orgy, right?"

Kathryn scoffed. "No, no orgy. It's just a place where people can bring their partners to socialize with friends and colleagues. The contracts just ensure that everyone plays by the rules and everyone is safe. Come on, Sofe. You need it. You need it. Come on."

"If it will get you off my back, fine. I'll go. There are worse places to spend Saturday night than a house on Whidbey Island."

Marion sent off the last of the non-disclosure agreements for the Whidbey Island event and checked her watch. She had just enough time to walk through the kitchen and make sure everything was on schedule, then walk to the trolley stop. NDAs weren't normal procedure, but they were frequent enough that she'd stopped complaining about them. Celebrities were very private people, and even if the thing they were trying to keep quiet was that they couldn't handle spicy food, Marion was more than happy to protect that secret with the full force of the law. Business had picked up recently. It seemed like there was an event every night. She and Courtney had to hire an entire new team just to handle all the calls, and the kitchen was constantly in use. The specter of Sofia Kennedy's Back-Up segment was a distant and practically forgotten memory.

Courtney came in as Marion was on her way out, and she stopped to hold the door for her. "Non-disclosures are sent off," Marion said. "Everything should be set. Can you work the party?"

"It's tomorrow night? I can't. I have that church brunch on Sunday. I need to be there by ten to set everything up."

"Right. Okay, I can take Oak Harbor."

"You sure? I can swap with someone else."

Marion nodded. "It'll be fine. I want you to head up that church thing. Everything else good?"

"Peachy," Courtney said. "Kyle told me old van was acting up again, so I rearranged the teams so we could have time to take it to a mechanic."

"Good looking out." She checked her watch again. "Okay, I need to go if I'm going to catch the trolley. Take care of the place."

"I'll do my best."

"You never do anything else. See you Monday."

She turned up her collar as she left the building and headed for the trolley stop. She fitted in her ear buds and listened to Corinne

Bailey Rae as she walked through the drizzle. She didn't plan to go home, instead riding the trolley to a bar she hadn't been to before. She and Penny had hooked up a couple times since their first encounter in Thigh High's parking lot, but neither of them wanted anything more permanent. The sex was great, but their personalities didn't match. Every interaction would be a repeat of their first dance: both of them moving to lead before one had to awkwardly retreat and follow.

Marion was feeling elated and invigorated, and she wanted to share that with someone. It was nearly midnight when she got to the bar. By one o'clock she was flirting with a redhead who, by one-thirty, offered her a ride home. They had sex, the redhead accepted Marion's invitation to spend the night, and in the morning made Marion breakfast before slipping out of the apartment. Marion ate the pancakes and drank the coffee while sitting in front of her window. She had a view of some downtown buildings, but she kept her focus on the tree-lined street between her building and the one across the street. The trees stretched across to each other and formed an almost unbroken canopy that gave the illusion of being in the woods. She liked that sensation, the idea of wilds in the urban jungle.

She spent the day cleaning her apartment. At noon she called to make sure everything was on track for the Oak Harbor party. The team leader she had assigned to the event was Tyrone, always reliable and a stickler for details. As expected, he had everything under control. They would leave two hours ahead of schedule to give themselves a bit of wiggle room in terms of traffic and ferry wait times, which means they should be out the door no later than three o'clock. Tyrone assured her the van would be waiting to leave by ten to three.

She ironed her uniform, the black dress shirt and slacks, and did her hair before she changed out of her pajamas. She watched herself in the mirror as she changed from sloppy and lazy to professional server. It was only recently she'd decided she didn't have to justify her presence at events. It was her prerogative to do every aspect of the job, and if that meant getting her hands dirty and standing around for hours on end, then no one would tell her she couldn't. Being the boss meant she could do whatever job she wanted at the company, no matter how far above it she supposedly was.

Marion winked at herself and made sure the knot in her white silk tie was perfect before grabbing her bag and heading out. Even if she missed the first trolley, she had time enough to wait for a second one to show up. She didn't want to jinx herself, but things had been going extremely well since the Sofia Kennedy hiccup. They lost a little business from a handful of clients, but they hadn't lost any of their momentum. With any luck, they were looking at their most profitable year ever.

Come to think of it, the Back-Up segment had lit a fire under her. She and Courtney had worked harder than ever to make sure their clients were left satisfied. That translated to good online reviews and word of mouth that led to more clients. She smiled as she realized she might actually owe Sofia Kennedy a thank-you note.

She laughed at the thought as she went downstairs. Somehow she doubted the day she thanked that woman was far, far in the future.

CHAPTER ELEVEN

DESPITE ASSURANCES of the party's level of discretion, Sofia tried to make sure she looked as different as possible from her TV persona. She chose a black blouse and a knee-length skirt, as far from the pantsuit-blazer combos she wore for the news. Her hair was grown out long enough for her to put it in an up-do, leaving her neck exposed and - according to Kathryn when she picked her up - accentuate her cheekbones. "Seriously, you look almost regal in that get-up." Sofia had rolled her eyes and complimented Kathryn on her own outfit before following her downstairs.

The drive to the island took over an hour with traffic. They passed the time with the *Hamilton* soundtrack for most of the ride, Sofia impressing Kathryn with her ability to sing along with Lafayette in 'Guns and Ships.' Kathryn did a passable version of King George, and neither of them even tried to sing along with 'It's Quiet Uptown.' By the time they boarded the ferry, Sofia was wondering if the party was even necessary. She felt more relaxed than she had in ages.

"Don't try backing out of it now," Kathryn warned. "You didn't get dressed up so fine just to waste it in my car. You're going to show yourself off."

Sofia sighed.

Kathryn drove them through the quaint town where the ferry

docked and then descended into the untamed wilds of the island's interior. Sofia checked her phone and saw that it wasn't getting a signal.

"You're taking me to a murder house, aren't you?"

"No," Kathryn said, "but at least you don't have to worry about pictures from the party showing up on Facebook or Instagram."

"Shame. The police might have been able to use that evidence to piece together the hours before we went missing."

"Shush. You're letting all that news you report get to you."

Sofia said, "How do you even know these people? If they're so adamant about security and privacy, then why the hell would they invite a journalist?"

"Because... th-they invited me..."

"But you're straight. Right?"

"I am." She was suddenly anxious, shifting in her seat and flexing her fingers on the steering wheel. "But when you came out, I started reading up on things. LGBT rights, marriage equality, all the things I'd sort of let slip because I didn't think they affected me. But once they did, I wanted to be informed."

Sofia glared at her. "You were researching a story."

"I was."

"Damn it, Kathryn."

"I would have kept you out of it. You know that. Gay rights are such a big issue, and things have been changing so rapidly after decades of stonewalling. Oh, Stonewall. I know what that is now."

Sofia rolled her eyes.

"I was nosing around, and someone I spoke with thought that I was personally invested. They told me about this party and suggested I check it out."

"Are there cameras in the car?" Sofia asked. "Are you planning to interview people once we get there?"

"No. Absolutely not. I may have found out about this party because of a story, but I would never betray anyone's secret. That's one thing I learned in my research, okay? People can only reveal themselves. No matter how much good I think I might be doing, it would only cause pain and heartache if I outed someone without their permission."

"Well, good for you," Sofia muttered.

Kathryn said, "We can skip it if you want. I'm sorry I didn't tell you."

"No." She sagged against the seat. "We've already come this far.

Might as well get it over with."

"That's the spirit." Kathryn reached over and patted Sofia's knee. "You're going to have a good time at this party. I guarantee it."

Sofia didn't say anything, but she was sure her body language conveyed the depths of her skepticism. After ten minutes of driving, Kathryn turned right, drove for another few minutes, then turned right again, and once more, bringing them onto narrower and more secluded roads each time. Sofia had gotten so turned around she wasn't entirely sure which direction the ferry dock was anymore.

"Yes. There is definitely a murder house at the end of this spiral."

"Will you hush? No one is murdering you tonight."

Sofia said, "If there is, I will haunt your ghost through the whole afterlife."

"Deal."

The trees which had been moving closer and closer to the sides of the car suddenly retreated to reveal a wide clearing that included a gorgeous cabin. There was a detached garage to one side and a sprawling patio between the two buildings with fairy lights and Chinese lanterns strung up to make it look like something out of a ridiculous rom-com.

"Some murder house, huh?"

Sofia said, "Okay, this does look pretty spectacular."

A man in a red jacket was standing at the edge of the clearing and smiled as he directed them to the right. Kathryn followed a dirt road around the garage to where Sofia estimated a dozen cars had been parked. As she maneuvered toward a spot, they passed a white van with a group of people unloading trays and covered dishes from the back. It was too dark to read the name written on the side of the van even if either of them had bothered to look.

Tyrone helped Lisa bring in the last of the zucchini sticks from the back of the van while Marion helped prepare trays in the kitchen. Baked clams, crudités, stuffed mushrooms. The drinks were ready to be handed out, but only after James and Tracy had made at least one circuit of the room with appetizers. They didn't want another fake food poisoning fiasco on their hands. They'd been at the house for over an hour making sure everything was ready to roll at party time. It had taken longer than she anticipated to find the house. James made a wrong turn and ended up on the other side of the island.

But eventually the entire crew had found the narrow, winding lane that led to their client's home. Now they were at T-minus however many seconds and she was making sure nothing had fallen through the cracks. Tyrone came over to her. "Everything's in. I spoke to the host and said we can start making the rounds whenever you're ready."

"Then let's get out there." She picked up a tray of apple tarts and joined Tracy at the kitchen door and gestured for her to lead the way.

Every surface of the main room seemed to be made of wood: floors, walls, and ceiling were all beautifully-stained and polished to reflect light from the chandelier. The stone fireplace was flanked on either side by shelves crammed full of books that appeared to have actually been read. To their left as they came out of the kitchen were the open doors to the patio where people had already started mingling. To the right was a partially-detached office area. Tracy went outside, Tyrone went straight ahead, and Marion went into the office.

There was only one guest in the office, a black-haired woman standing at the window gazing out at the trees. The sun had gone down but the property was lit well enough to show off how beautiful the area was. Marion cleared her throat and said, "Could I interest you in~" Her voice caught in her throat as the woman turned to reveal her identity. "It's you."

Sofia Kennedy chuckled quietly and closed her eyes. "Of course it's you."

They stood silently for a long moment. Marion didn't think fleeing was the right option, and she could tell Sofia was struggling with the same dilemma. They were adults. Running away from each other was childish. But the longer they stood facing one another across the room, the more necessary it would become for one of them to break the silence. Marion shifted her weight and looked at the tray she was carrying on one flat hand.

"Could I, ah, interest you in an apple tart?"

Sofia took a breath and exhaled slowly. "Sure. I love apples." She rounded the desk and took one of the tarts from the tray.

"Can't have you drinking on an empty stomach, can we?"

Sofia snapped her eyes back up to meet Marion's as she took a bite. When she determined Marion was just making a joke, she let the corners of her mouth tick up slightly. She chewed carefully and swallowed before she responded.

"No. Wouldn't want history to repeat itself." Sofia looked past Marion into the party. "So this is your company. You seem to have bounced back well from my segment."

"Yeah. Guess you don't have as much influence as you thought."

Sofia arched an eyebrow.

"Sorry. That was mean."

"No, no. It was certainly... in line with our previous encounters."

Marion said, "Oh, if that's what we're aiming for, I could toss the rest of these apple tarts in your face."

Sofia hesitated with the tart halfway to her mouth. "You wouldn't."

"God no. Do you know how long it took to make these?"

Sofia managed an authentic smile for that. "I appreciate your restraint. They are quite good. May I?" She reached for another and Marion moved the tray closer. "So you signed the..."

"The contract to keep my mouth shut about this party? Sure. They're not that unusual in this line of work."

"Mm-hmm," Sofia said, averting her gaze.

Marion looked into the party. "I should give everyone else a chance to get their hands on these. I'll try to get back around to you before they're completely gone."

"I'd appreciate that."

Marion nodded and backed out of the room. A man instantly made his way over to her and asked what was on her tray. As she explained it she saw Sofia leave the office and cross to the deck. She paused on the threshold for a moment to scan the crowd before she went outside to join them. Marion was glad their encounter had been civil. The tenuous peace made it easier for her to admit that the anchorwoman, beautiful on an ordinary day, had turned into an absolute knockout for the party. She tore her gaze away, refusing to be distracted by her erstwhile nemesis. Their feud was in the past, they had made as many amends as they were ever likely to make, and it was time to move on.

She carried the tray to the next person.

"You're not going to believe who is here," Sofia hissed next to Kathryn's ear.

"I know," Kathryn said. "I saw him, too. It makes me feel better that you didn't know he was gay. I thought my gaydar was off."

"No, not h~ and your gaydar is shit if it didn't pick up on me after all these years." She eyed the young African-American man offering zucchini sticks to one of the other groups on the patio. She waited until he was out of earshot before she continued. "Do you know who is catering this thing?"

Kathryn looked around at the waiters. "Should I?"

"Beacon Craft & Catering Service."

Her eyes widened. "Oh. Is she...?"

"She is. I just ran into her. She offered me an apple tart."

Kathryn turned to look into the main room. "Ooh, that sounds fantastic."

"Can you focus?"

"What? Did you guys argue?"

"No. No, actually it was very civil."

"So...?"

Sofia sighed, "I don't know. It just put my guard up. I didn't expect to see anyone I knew here, and for it to be *her*... after everything that happened between us earlier this year..."

Kathryn rubbed Sofia's arm. "Do you want to go home?"

"No. That wouldn't be fair to you."

"I'm here for you, kid. You want to go, we'll go. After I get one of those apple tarts."

Sofia smiled. "We can stick around. I'll just avoid anyone in a black shirt and white tie. I'll come find you if it gets to be too much. I promise."

"Good."

"And for the record, who were you talking about earlier?" Kathryn turned to look into the room, leveling her gaze at someone near the front door. She used her chin to point without pointing. Sofia's eyes widened when she saw the popular hockey player holding hands with a man. "Okay, wow. No shame for not seeing that one coming."

They split up again. Sofia had already greeted the host and thanked him for inviting her, but she didn't feel like socializing with anyone else. She had never been particularly good at small talk. Reggie used to cover that for her. She also used to put her hand on the back of Sofia's neck and drew the tip of her middle finger from Sofia's hair down to her collar, following her spine down to the collar of whatever top she was wearing.

Only Sofia and Reggie knew the secret meaning behind the

touch. The first time they had sex, Reggie had put her hand under Sofia's hair and drew that same line as her other hand was busy between Sofia's legs. Sofia had smiled up at her.

"What are you doing?"

"Planning for the future."

Afterward, every time they made love, at some point Reggie would reach up and touch her there. A few strokes, from the nape of her neck down to her shoulders. Sometimes one stroke, sometimes a full-on petting. She never explained herself until one night when they made plans to see a movie together. Sofia was waiting on the corner, looking at her phone, worrying they wouldn't get good seats if Reggie didn't get there soon. Reggie snuck up on her from behind and stroked her from the nape of her neck to the collar of her shirt.

By then, that particular touch had created a Pavlovian response. Sofia's eyes closed, she shivered, and she felt instantly aroused as she turned around to see her partner's evil smile.

"Oh, that is *cruel...*"

"Come on," Reggie said, "we want to get good seats."

After that, Reggie would occasionally sneak in a quick touch while they were at dinner, when they were driving somewhere, or if she helped Sofia into her jacket. She got to the point where she could execute the move like a magician, obvious only to herself and Sofia. Every time Sofia had the same reaction. She would squeeze her thighs together or hiss through her teeth, and she would narrow her eyes and call Reggie the nastiest name she could think of. And Reggie would only grin and giggle like a schoolgirl caught at a prank. It was only tolerable because Reggie never waited very long to take care of the fire she'd started. Sofia resisted the urge to mimic the touch herself. The party was difficult enough without adding arousal to the mix. But once she got home...

She smiled to herself and continued to weave through the crowd.

CHAPTER TWELVE

THE PARTY began showing signs of waning at eleven-thirty, and the host quietly informed Marion they could stop serving and start packing their things up to go. At midnight they were still quite a way from being done, but one of the vans was fully-packed and ready to go. Marion made the executive decision to let everyone on the team go home so they could catch the ferry. They would be getting home in the middle of the night as it was, and she didn't want to make it any worse for them. Of course, once they were gone, she realized she would have to pack and clean by herself and wondered if being the boss was really all it was cracked up to be.

"Hey…"

She looked up and saw Sofia poking her head through the door. "Hey."

"Can I come in?"

"It's not my kitchen anymore."

Sofia grinned and slid the rest of the way inside. She let the door shut behind her. She was swaying on her feet but still capable of moving in a straight line. Almost. Despite the flush in her cheeks from the alcohol and the slight mussing of her hair, she was still as gorgeous as she'd been at the beginning of the night. It wasn't fair. A celebrity should have been shorter or less attractive in real life. It didn't make sense that the camera somehow dimmed Sofia's natural beauty, but it certainly seemed to be the case.

"I was told you might have some more wine bouncing around. So I thought I'd save you from having to crate it up and tote it back to the mainland."

Marion gestured to the counter next to the stove. "There might be a bottle of cabernet over there you can kill off for me."

"Much obliged." She went over and retrieved a glass.

Marion watched her without raising her head from what she was doing. "So... good party?"

"It was all right. The booze was top-shelf." She chuckled, a husky sound, and lifted her newly-filled glass in a toast. "My compliments to the chef. You have indeed redummed yourself in my eyes." She cleared her throat. "Redeemed. You have redeemed yourself."

"Are you sure you haven't already had enough?"

"Mm, I'm not driving. Whose brilliant idea was it to have a party way the hell out here? With a ferry involved. And a... bridge." She took a drink and approached the table. "What are you doing?"

"Loading the trays into the van so I can head back. Look, why don't I help you find your friend? She can put you in the car and you can start sleeping this off."

Sofia sighed heavily and rolled her head to the side to look at Marion. "She would have liked you."

"Who? Your friend?" She remembered seeing the Native reporter hanging around the party with Sofia.

"Mm-mm." She emphatically shook her head, like a child protesting her bedtime. "No. Reggie."

"Who is Reggie?"

Sofia ignored the question. "She would have loved you. You stood your ground. Even if you insulted her."

"When did I—"

"Sh, sh." She came around the edge of the table. "You're tough and you don't take any bullshit. And you look good in a tie. Damn good, woman."

She suddenly sagged. Marion said, "Whoop..." and grabbed her around the waist to keep her upright. Sofia put her hands on Marion's shoulders to steady herself. Marion kept her hands on Sofia's hips just in case she swayed again. "You okay, Miss Kennedy?"

"Hum," Sofia said, and then kissed Marion. Marion yelped against Sofia's mouth, and Sofia responded by pressing her tongue against Marion's teeth. Marion backed away but Sofia followed. She grabbed hold of Marion's tie just under the knot and tilted her head to change the angle of their kiss, and Marion looked toward the door. She didn't know if she was looking for help or to make sure no one would catch her. Either way, the door remained stubbornly - or fortuitously - closed.

Sofia ended the kiss by brushing her tongue over Marion's lips. She said, "Hum," again and then shifted her weight to lean her hip against the counter. "Whoa."

Marion's face was burning, her ears surely hot to the touch. Sofia put a hand over her mouth and focused on a spot somewhere on the floor behind Marion. The kitchen door finally opened and Sofia's friend stuck her head in.

"Oh. Hey, Sofe... everything okay in here?"

"Everything's fine." Sofia cleared her throat and stood up straighter, forcing herself to be steady. "You did a lovely job this evening, Miss Vog-ut. Voot." She screwed up her lips and said, "Vogt."

Marion nodded. "Sure." Her voice was small, choked. "Sure thing, Miss Kennedy."

Kathryn looked between them both and raised an eyebrow. "Okay... well, since no one is bleeding, I'm going to assume nothing bad happened. Sofe, you ready to go?"

"Mm-hmm." She walked around the table and swayed a bit as she walked to her friend's side. "I hope to eat you again soon."

Marion said, "What?"

"Tarts," Sofia said. "Apple tarts. The... the tarts. They were delicious." She put her arm around her friend's waist. "I think I'll sleep in the backseat on the drive home, Kathryn."

Kathryn said, "Yeah, I think that's a pretty good idea." She looked over her shoulder at Marion as she guided Sofia out of the kitchen, still looking perplexed as the door shut behind her.

Marion, left alone in the kitchen, finally let out the breath she'd been holding. She put her hands in her hair, scratched her scalp, and looked at all the work she still had left. Work. Packing away her supplies. That would get her mind off the insanity that had just occurred. She cleared her throat, nodded to herself, and focused on cleaning up.

Kathryn parked in front of Sofia's building at a little past one-thirty in the morning. She helped her friend upstairs and let her into the dark apartment.

"Okay, Sofe, here we are. Safe and sound. Do you need anything before I go?"

"No, hey, don't go back out. It's the middle of the night. Stay here. You can crash on the couch."

Kathryn looked at the couch with obvious longing. It only took a few seconds for the potential discomfort to win out over the thought of going back out and driving home. She borrowed a shirt from Sofia and went to change. Sofia went into the bedroom and sat on the bed to take off her shoes, let her hair down, and struggle out of the "fancy clothes" she'd worn to the party.

She thought about how the experiences solidified into memories, like a Polaroid slowly fading from nothing into a perfect image. Only memories were reversed: it went from a crystal clear memory into something milkier. Solid but open to interpretation. She thought of the faces of people she'd spoken with, the layout of the house, the view off the patio, Marion's face...

"Oh, shit," she said, rubbing a hand over her face. "Nice move, Sofe. God, what were you thinking?"

"You were right, you know," Reggie said.

Sofia realized she had fallen asleep sitting up. "About?"

"I do like her."

Sofia snorted. "You would."

Reggie laughed. "She challenges you. She wouldn't let you get away with sitting around an empty apartment feeling sorry for yourself for three years."

"She tastes good." She grunted. "Her food. I meant her food..."

"Sure you did, sweetheart," Reggie said.

Sofia sighed and slumped over. She waited for Reggie to cover her up and, realizing the futility of that, reached down and tugged the blanket into place herself.

"Ignore everything else if you want to," Reggie's voice whispered in her head as she settled against the pillow, "the circumstances say that should've been an awful kiss. But it wasn't... was it?"

Sofia's face slumped into a smile as she drifted off. Her hand drifted to her chest, stroking the curve of her breast as her mind raced about what might have happened if she hadn't been drunk. If she'd given Marion a chance, would she have said no? The opportunity was gone for good, but that wouldn't keep her from speculating about what she'd missed out on.

Marion didn't get home until after three o'clock. She missed the last ferry off the island and had to drive the full length of Whidbey Island to Deception Bridge. It added more than an hour to her return trip, but at least the roads were relatively empty for the entire trip. She blasted music to keep awake and tried not to think about the kiss. It was a drunken collision and nothing more. Odds were good that Sofia wouldn't even remember it come morning.

She drove the van home and sent an email to Courtney so she wouldn't freak out if she noticed it missing in the morning. When she had a few hours of sleep in the bank she would take the van back to the office and unload everything. That was the benefit of being in charge, she realized. She could borrow the company vehicles without permission and all the dishes were someone else's responsibility.

She didn't bother turning on her apartment's lights, sitting on the edge of her bed to take off her shoes. The relief when her feet were freed was almost orgasmic, and she sighed as she flexed her toes and dropped back onto the mattress. Her clothes were still on and she still smelled of the party and the van, a disgusting mixture of all the food she and her team had spent the past few days preparing. But the host had been thrilled with it. He asked for her card and, before she left, he gave her a huge cash tip that she would distribute to the team in the morning. She reached up to loosen her tie so it wouldn't choke her in the night and remembered how it had felt to have Sofia Kennedy grabbing it. How it felt to have Sofia Kennedy's mouth on hers. She swept her tongue across her lips as if she could retroactively return the kiss. What if she had responded in the moment? Would Sofia have started undressing her? Would they have stumbled into the fridge and would Sofia have gotten on her knees and would she have~

"Fuuuuuu..." Marion grunted, cutting off the curse before it could finish. She forced herself to sit up and groggily undressed. Sofia was drunk. She was just being overly affectionate or displaying lousy judgment or... whatever. It hadn't meant anything. Even if she couldn't stop thinking about it. She reached down and unbuckled her pants, eyes closed as if she was trying to fool herself into thinking she was unconscious.

She imagined a different scenario playing out, one where she returned Sofia's kiss. She imagined a chain of events where they hadn't been interrupted and their clothes fell to the nice tile floor of the host's kitchen. And then she would have gotten down onto the pile of her discarded uniform, her underwear around her thighs as Sofia got on top of her. She'd never had sex with a celebrity before. Even if it was a celebrity she didn't particularly like.

With two fingers flat against the cotton of her underwear, she half-imagined and half dreamed Sofia turning her around. In the dream, Marion, hands flat on the table, arched her back and pressed her ass into Sofia's hips. Sofia brushed Marion's blonde braid to one side and bowed to kiss her neck as she wrapped both arms around Marion's waist. In bed, Marion worried her bottom lip with her teeth as she imagined being pinned between Sofia and the table, trapped, helpless, unable to escape and unwilling to even try.

She imagined Sofia's breath on her ear. Her voice was east coast, refined without being quiet British. Her teeth cut off the crisp consonants and her tongue curled around the vowels, and thoughts of what that talented mouth could do to her body made parts of Marion's body tingle with anticipation.

"Would you like me to stop, Miss Vogt?"

"No," she said aloud to her empty room. She raised her hips and moved her hand between her legs to cup herself as she imagined Sofia would have. "Don't stop," she said as she touched herself.

She could almost hear the brush of her uniform slacks against the material of Sofia's dress and the clanking of trays as her grip tightened on the edge of the table. Her breathing became rougher as she put her free hand on her breast, gripping it tightly.

"Too rough, Miss Vogt?"

"Harder," Marion grunted.

Sofia's laugh would be throaty, a superior growl, and Marion whimpered. Sofia wouldn't have been gentle, so Marion allowed herself to get rough. She writhed under her own hand, moving her legs further apart.

"Make me come, Sofia."

"Ask nicely, Miss Vogt, and maybe I'll let you."

She shivered and wished she'd actually heard that demanding voice purr those words in her ear. "Please, Sofia."

"Good girl."

Marion cried out when she came, closing her thighs around her hand as she twitched and jerked through her climax. Her face was flush again as she rolled onto her side. She chuckled softly to herself and shook her head. A month ago she still would have called Sofia Kennedy her nemesis. Now she had graduated to fantasy fodder.

The line between fury and lust really could be frightfully thin sometimes. She scooted higher on the mattress and pulled the pillow down, wrapping one arm around it as she burrowed her face into the silky soft pillowcase and drifted off to a peaceful post-orgasmic sleep.

CHAPTER THIRTEEN

THE ROAR of the interstate was almost a physical force, a solid wall of sound that made it difficult to hear as Sofia followed the men through the underbrush just beyond the park. She looked back to make sure her cameraman was following her. She had her phone in one hand, microphone in the other, and the KCTV cap kept the rain from getting in her eyes as they emerged into the clearing of the greenbelt. The ground ended in a cliff about twenty yards ahead, the drop-off protected by a chain-link fence. Just beyond it she could see cars, trucks, and semis flowing north on I-5 through the heart of the city.

Something cracked underfoot and she glanced down to see a broken syringe. Half a dozen more were scattered around on the gravel, along with foil and plastic spoons. This paraphernalia was the reason she was wearing heavy-duty boots, two pairs of pants, two gloves, and three layers of shirts: her blouse, her jacket, and a windbreaker. She didn't want to risk getting pricked or scraped by any of the debris left behind in this godforsaken strip of land.

The men they were with were ordinary citizens who were taking it upon themselves to clean up areas frequented by homeless junkies. This particular greenbelt was supposed to be inaccessible to the public due to the dangerous proximity to the road and the risk of people jumping the flimsy barrier and plummeting ten or fifteen feet into traffic, but obviously the homeless had found a way.

"Cody," she said to her cameraman, "get some footage along this gravel area. I want to make sure people see how littered this place is."

The leader of their escort had a twenty-eight-ounce plastic jug to fill with the trash they found. In the truck she'd thought it was overkill, but it was already starting to run out of room and they still had the length of a city block to cover.

Cody finished filming the b-roll and moved closer, raising his voice to be heard over the rumble of engines. "We're going to have to record at the perfect time, otherwise no one will be able to hear a word you're saying."

"Yeah. Hopefully this is just rush hour. It might die down soon. If it comes down to it, I can just do the whole thing in voiceover. Be sure you get enough footage if we have to go that route."

He nodded and moved off to film the rest of the area. The police had cleared out the encampment a few days earlier, but the city couldn't spare the manpower to come down and clean up everything that had been left behind. That was where community volunteers like Jerry Rogen and his six helpers came in. They found out where the camps had been and came out to do a quick, efficient, safe cleanup.

The purpose of Sofia's report was to shine a light on the city's drug and homeless problem while also drawing attention to the good deeds of Jerry and his friends. It was a different take on the Back-Up segment, moving away from calling out wrongdoers and instead showing the people who were helping to make Seattle better. She would still confront con artists and cheats, but she wanted to combine those stories with pieces like this, pieces that showed selflessness and generosity of time and spirit.

Her producer called it a "kinder, gentler" version of Back-Up, but she disagreed. It was what she'd originally wanted for the project, what it started out as. Her experience with Marion Vogt had shown her how far from center she had gone. The majority of the time she went after definite cheats, people who had taken money for promised work that was never completed. That's not what Reggie had wanted the segment to be. She wanted it to be about helping out fellow citizens.

There was a lull in traffic and she signaled for Cody to begin filming. She kept her cap on rather than risk the wind blowing hair into her face. When Cody signaled her, she said, "Right now, we're standing in a greenbelt just north of Yesler Way, right above the interstate as you can probably hear. This area is closed off to the public, but until recently it was home to a community of homeless addicts. These men and women were recently moved to various shelters and clinics, but they left this behind."

Cody aimed the camera down and panned along the edge of the gravel.

"Broken bottles, syringes, foil, and plastic spoons used for administering drugs. It's up to the city to make sure all this debris and hazardous waste is gathered, but there are just too many of these campsites for anyone to keep up. But trying to take on a bit of the effort is Jerry Rogen and his crew." She moved closer to where Jerry was gathering trash. "Jerry and his team of six or seven helpers choose to come out here on their day off, risking infection or injury to make sure that their city is safe for everyone. Jerry, can we take a second?"

"Sure can." He placed a syringe in his jar, made sure the lid was screwed on tight, and moved to stand next to her in-frame. "Hi, Sofia."

"Hi, Jerry." She pointed at the jar with her small finger. "Now, this is just what you've gathered in the past ten minutes. The jar is practically full."

"It is. This is all kinds of drug paraphernalia and other trash. The broken bottles and whatnot might not have drug residue on them, but they'd be just as likely to cause you some sort of injury. And you get a nice rain, this place will flood and all these needles will go out onto the I-5. Kind of a nasty surprise to find in the back of your pickup truck or your boat."

"Absolutely. How many of these jugs do you typically fill during an excursion like this?"

"Well, this particular greenbelt here is fairly long. We call this a four-jugger because we'll fill up four of these bad boys."

Sofia said, "Wow, unbelievable. Now, have any of your people ever been hurt doing this?"

"Well, I'd say no, but we've had a few bumps and bruises. Greg twisted his ankle coming down a slope about a year ago, and we've got the normal bumps and bruises. No one has ever been pricked by a needle or needed to be checked out by a hospital, but we've got all their numbers on all our speed-dials just in case."

Sofia smiled. "Let's hope you never have to use them, Jerry. I'll let you get back to work here." She moved to one side and faced the camera again. The traffic noise was building once more, so she raised her voice to match it. "Ordinary men and women putting their health and safety at risk to make Seattle better, cleaner, and safer for everyone else. Lately this segment has been about having me act as backup when you need a hand, but that's not what it should be about. It should focus on people like this, people who are out there providing backup without the glamour. If you know of someone who is providing backup - whether for one person or the entire city - get in touch with us. For KCTV 6, and for Jerry Rogen and his team of cleaners, I'm Sofia Kennedy. Back to you, Del."

Sofia stayed for a bit to help Jerry's team but she had to beg off long before they were done so she could get back to the studio. It felt good to walk away from a story knowing she might have helped without attacking anyone, without a confrontation.

She knew Reggie would've been proud of her for the story, prouder than she would've been after any of the other Back-Up segments aired. She would have smiled, she would have said, "That's wonderful, Sofe." She would have been happy for the victims who got justice, but now Sofia could see that she'd become a villain to a lot of people. She descended on them from out of the blue wielding one mistake from the past, and she had crucified them for it. She was ready to stop being the villain.

On the drive back to the studio, she thought about her drunken encounter with Marion. She was mortified the next morning when she woke up and remembered the kiss. After administering a hangover cure and taking a long, thorough shower, she considered calling to apologize. The kiss had been yet another in a series of unwelcome advances on the caterer. She would be lucky if she didn't get Maced the next time they ran into each other.

Still, what a kiss. Even through the haze of being drunk and the less than ideal situation, she remembered the kiss being something special. She was more than a little sad they wouldn't get a chance to do it again properly. Who knows what it might have been like if Marion had kissed her back. She knew Marion was at least on the right side of the sexual spectrum; she had a MEOW account, after all. Sofia remembered seeing the app on Marion's phone during their brief gym encounter.

A thought occurred to her, but she waited until she was at the semi-privacy of her desk before she acted on it. She used her phone so there wouldn't be a record on her work laptop and looked around to be positive no one else was close enough to see her screen before she went to the site. She had deleted her former account, so she had to fill out a new profile. She chose a profile photo that kept most of her face obscured by the upturned collar of her coat, her hair covered by a knit cap so only one eye and the bridge of her nose was showing. She remembered Kathryn saying she looked regal at the party, so she chose "S_Queen" as her user name. She put self-employed under profession, kept her age and location true, and logged in.

She wondered what name Marion would use for her profile. Beacon? Something to do with food or catering? She searched for VogtCaters and came up empty. She tried Maid Marion, though she didn't seem the type, and was proven correct. It would almost be better if she couldn't find her. It would put an end to her fantasy of...

The search results had taken her to a page with multiple rows of profiles, and her gaze happened to land on "MVP_Chef." The profile picture showed her with slightly darker hair and sunglasses, the finer details of her face were obscured by a burst of sunlight, but once she started looking she could tell it was definitely Marion. *MVP... Marion Vogt. Wonder what the P stands for.*

She clicked on the profile and saw that Marion was a few years younger than her, interested in a relationship or casual friendship with women between thirty and forty, and her hobbies included hiking, swimming, and reading. No smokers, some drinking was okay, et cetera and so forth. There were pictures that Sofia scrolled through and discovered Marion Vogt was indeed very attractive. She could smile, something she had yet to do in Sofia's presence, but Sofia felt maybe there was a reason for that.

"Oh my God," Kathryn gasped from behind her, prompting Sofia to risk dropping the phone as she slapped it face-down on the desk. Kathryn moved around to sit next to Sofia's desk. "Too late. I saw it. You're on the dating app. Do you have a profile?"

"I... no, I'm not... I saw someone with it and I thought..." She scratched her cheek and pushed her hair off her forehead. "I'm just, for a story, about dating apps..."

Kathryn said, "I know what app you were using. I recognized the color scheme."

Sofia said, "It's not a big deal. I was just seeing what it was like."

"Okay. Sure. I'll pretend to go along with that, for now. But if you meet anyone, I want to be your sounding board."

"You're going to judge anyone I date anyway."

"Mm-hmm." Kathryn bumped Sofia's foot with hers. "That's not why I came over here. I came over here to get your lunch plans."

Sofia said, "I have no lunch plans. What do you have in mind?"

"Mexican?"

"I can do Mexican."

"Great." She slapped her hand on Sofia's leg. "And while we're eating you can tell me what happened with the caterer at the party."

Kathryn tried to make a hasty retreat, but Sofia's legs were longer. She caught up with her friend and detoured her into the kitchenette. Kathryn was chuckling under her breath.

"What are you talking about?"

"What do you mean? I saw the two of you."

Sofia's face reddened. "No. No, I was in the kitchen, and I got the rest of the cabernet, and then I, I went outside and you drove me home." She tried to remember where she'd run into Kathryn after she left the kitchen but couldn't make the memory come forth. She'd made the choice to leave the kitchen and break the kiss, hadn't she? Or had she just stopped kissing Marion because they were caught?

"When you came into the kitchen, were we...?

"You weren't actually doing anything. But your blocking was conspicuous as hell. If you weren't doing something, you were about to." She leaned in closer. "Did something happen? Or did I stop something from happening?"

Sofia looked into the newsroom. She wished there was someone around so she could beg off the conversation, but every desk was vacant. Kathryn caught her desperate scan.

"Okay. We're at work, so I won't push you to talk about it. But we'll get something take-out, eat it at my apartment, and I want details then."

"Fine," Sofia said.

Kathryn rubbed Sofia's arms. "I hope you know I'm only pushing because I want you to be happy. I want to live vicariously through your lame domestic life."

Sofia said, "I know." She kissed Kathryn's cheek. "But you're still a pain in the ass snoop."

"We all have our roles to play. I'll swing by in about half an hour and we'll head out."

Sofia agreed and went back to her desk, suddenly very aware she'd left the screen on and open to a lesbian dating app. The room may have been empty and the phone facedown, but she still felt a surge of panic at what might have happened. She retrieved the phone and looked at Marion's profile again. There was a picture of her leaning against a railing with the Seattle Aquarium behind her. The shadow of the Ferris wheel was falling on her. She was wearing a grey cardigan over a button-down blouse with a scarf loosely draped over her shoulders. Her hair was longer, hanging in wild curls over her right shoulder.

In another situation, if they'd met under different circumstances, Sofia admitted she would find Marion gorgeous. Maybe that was what prompted the kiss. Maybe the alcohol had been enough to push through all the context and get to what she really wanted to do. And god, it needed to be repeated, it had been a damned good kiss. It had been so good she almost wanted to do it again just to see if it had been a fluke.

But to do it again would require setting up a deliberate meeting. She couldn't count on fate and happenstance to bring them together again. Fate had done enough work; it was up to her now. The profile had an option to send a Purr, and she hesitated before clicking on it. She might only get one chance at contacting Marion. What if the message was buried under other Purrs? She would never know if Marion had chosen to ignore the note or if she'd just never seen it.

Then again, she had the benefit of anonymity. She didn't have to identify herself right away. She clicked on Purr at Her and turned the phone so she could use both thumbs on the keyboard that popped up. She typed, "I've had your food. Beacon Craft and Catering? It's delicious! I appreciate a woman who knows her way around a kitchen." She added a winking emoji.

"For crying out loud," she muttered as she hit 'send.' "What are you, a teenager?"

No matter how embarrassing, the damage had been done and she couldn't take it back. She closed the browser, stuck her phone in her pocket, and went to see if she could convince Kathryn to take an earlier lunch.

Chapter Fourteen

Marion showered and dressed for bed in shorts and a tank top. She wanted to read for a while before going to sleep, but first she checked her MEOW app to see if she'd gotten any new messages. She smiled when she saw one from someone called S_Queen, pondering what the "S" might stand for. She opened the profile and sighed at the picture that didn't tell her anything about what this "queen" might look like. That was fine, though. She had gorgeous eyes. No other pictures, a sparse profile, but the message had been polite and accurate enough that she didn't feel like it was spam or a bot. She went back and opened a reply box.

"That's us! Thank you so much! Hopefully you'll think of us for your next event. Your profile is kind of bare, Queenie. New to the site?"

Sofia was brushing her teeth when her phone chimed. She kept the brush in her mouth as she went out to check it, already dressed for bed in her faded scarlet nightgown. She touched the screen and saw the notification was from MEOW, and her eyes widened when she saw who it was from. "Oh fuff," she said around her mouthful of spearmint froth. She went back to the bathroom and considered her response as she rinsed. Should she come clean immediately? Would that slam the brakes on the whole conversation? And if it didn't, did she risk making Marion angry when the truth was discovered?

She sat on the bed and bent her knees to create a table. She stared at the phone for a full minute until the screen dimmed, then she tapped it again and began writing.

"Pretty new. I just joined today. I'm still not sure I'm going to stick around but I wanted to test the waters a little."

Marion picked up her phone when it chimed again, laying aside her Kindle. She smiled at the response from Queen. She could guide the conversation toward dirty talk. Have a nice quickie before going to sleep. But that seemed too predatory and gross, and she didn't want Queen to think it was that sort of website. She stared at the wall as she considered what she would write back instead of the trite "What are you wearing?" After a moment she began typing.

Marion sent: "And you chose me out of all the 'eligible outstanding women' in Seattle? What an honor! Test the waters? Is that a joke because I said I was into swimming?"

Sofia had propped the pillow up behind her back. "No, slip of the tongue, I promise. I swim as well." She thought for a second and then decided she didn't have anything else to add. She could have ended the ruse right then and there by saying they'd seen each other in the pool before, then reveal her identity, but she couldn't bring herself to potentially end the conversation so quickly.

Marion replied quickly. "Well, that's something we have in common. I hope I didn't wake you up with my reply. It's pretty late."

"It is, but I was awake anyway. I was just getting ready for bed. You?"

"In bed," came the short reply.

Sofia stared at the screen and twisted her lips, tilting her head one way and then the other as she debated what it could mean.

After thirty seconds: "Not implying anything." Winking emoji.

Sofia blushed and sent back, "No, of course not." She drummed her fingers on the back of her phone. Her ears were burning. "What do you wear to bed?"

"Shit," she said out loud. "What are you doing, Sofia?"

Marion raised an eyebrow as she read the new message. She had been slouching but now she sat up, using her feet to move the blankets out of the way. If there was a chance of this going where it seemed to be going, she wanted to be able to spread out a little. She flipped her hair over her shoulder and considered lying. Lingerie, something slinky with more lace than actual cloth, but in the end she went with the truth.

"A white tank top and boyshorts. You?"

"Wow," Sofia muttered under her breath. She kept a glass of water by the bed and she reached for it to take a sip as she considered the seemingly-innocent question at the end of the note. Was she wearing what she was really wearing, or did she want to be wearing something else for Marion's imagination? And what did she care about Marion's imagination anyway? It wasn't like they were going to do anything. Were they? Did people do that sort of thing on this app? She took another sip of water and used one hand to type her response.

"A red nightgown. There was a bit of lace on the hem, but it got torn about a year ago. It's too comfortable to throw out and I haven't gotten around to fixing it."

Marion could picture it perfectly. She sucked her bottom lip into her mouth and held the phone up to type.

"Very nice. But it's not fair that you have all my pictures, but all I have is your eye. Give me an idea of who I'm talking to here."

This was the moment of truth, Sofia thought. They were so far down the path to awkwardness that she dreaded the reaction when Marion found out who she was talking to. She'd already forced a kiss on the poor woman. How could she do *this* under false pretenses as well. She closed her eyes, sighed, and opened her photo album. She scrolled past photos she'd taken for work, portraits she'd taken of Kathryn, various crap she'd seen around Seattle, and finally found a selfie. She was wearing her KCTV windbreaker, her hair down, smiling brightly into the lens. She let out a slow breath and sent the picture with no caption, no explanation, nothing.

Marion's smile faded when the image appeared. "What the hell?" She stared at Sofia Kennedy's smiling face and tried to figure out what it meant. Did S_Queen want to role-play? Was she using a photo grabbed off a Google search and trying to pass it off as herself? Or... S_Queen? Sofia... She dropped the phone onto the mattress. There was no way. There was absolutely no way it was really Sofia Kennedy on the other end of those messages. She would have seen Marion's face on the profile, she would have absolutely known who she was talking to when she sent the first message. So if it was her, was she playing some kind of game?

Oh, god, she had been mocking her. There was probably a crowd of anchors and weather-people gathered around the phone having a good laugh at the stupid caterer who tried to have cybersex with someone on a dating app called MEOW, for Christ's sake. She covered her face with both hands. She was humiliated. She was furious. Her phone chimed again. She turned her head, hand across her mouth, and glared at the screen.

"I'm sorry."

She scoffed and put her head down again. Another chime. And then another. When she looked she saw, "Are you still there?" and "Please don't be embarrassed."

She grabbed the phone. "Embarrassed? I'm PISSED OFF." She jabbed 'send' and let the phone drop back onto the mattress. When the phone chimed again she muttered a curse under her breath. She almost turned the damn thing off and went to bed, but curiosity got the better of her.

"I didn't want to lie about who I was. But I didn't want you to immediately slam the door in my face, either. I didn't know the right time to reveal who I was. I'm sorry."

"Why?" She sent the single word back, deciding to let Sofia interpret what it meant.

"Because I can't stop thinking about what it was like to kiss you."

Marion held her phone in both hands, glaring at the screen. She was embarrassed about how close she had come to being completely vulnerable with someone who had attacked her at every turn. But she seemed to be honestly trying to make amends. If the grudge was going to continue, it would be up to Marion to keep it going. She didn't want to do that. She didn't want to hate someone just to hate them. She closed her eyes and took a long, slow breath. For the past five months, every mention of Sofia Kennedy had caused her to sneer, to mutter under her breath, or change the channel to a different news station. She let those emotions go and opened her eyes.

"It wasn't the worst kiss I've ever had."

Sofia smiled, relieved after the long silence that the response wasn't full of cursing and angry rebukes. "Not the worst," she said softly to herself. "I guess I can live with that. The conditions were far from ideal, after all." But how to follow-up? The flirtation they'd fallen into was pretty much dead, but there was a chance they could revive it with enough mutual effort. She started to type twice before she scrapped her thought and deleted everything. On the third attempt, she forced herself to finish what she was writing and sent it before she could think better of it.

"I think you need time to deal with the fact of who you've been talking to. And it's late. So can we put a pin in this and talk later?"

Marion sighed. It was the perfect out. If she decided it was too bizarre or their history was too much to overcome, she could just ignore any further attempts at communication. Or the alternative...

"I think that would be a good idea. Goodnight, Sofia."

Sofia sent back, "Goodnight, Miss Vogt."

She closed the app and put the phone on the charger. Imagine, a civil conversation with Sofia Kennedy. Wonders truly never ceased.

Sofia got out of bed and went to the window. In the building across the alley she could see a woman doing yoga in front of the television and a couple having a very late dinner at their kitchen counter. Beyond the building she could see more headlights and taillights of people still on their way home or venturing out into the evening.

When she was falling in love with Reggie, everything had clicked so perfectly that it seemed like fate was pulling their strings. They found an amazing apartment they could afford, they had what Sofia considered the perfect balance between fighting and making up, and their taste for food and drink overlapped just enough that the fridge wasn't a battleground. It was the storybook love, the kind of easy romance that everyone hoped for but rarely got.

And then there were her bizarre feelings for Marion, a woman she set out to destroy after their first meeting. Once she forgave Marion for the inadvertent insults, her emotions almost immediately shifted to admiration and... maybe even attraction. She couldn't deny that she felt an eager twinge when she thought their online exchange was going to result in dirty talk and mutual masturbation. It was clear that what they were doing wasn't just her normal flirtation leading to a one-night stand. If all she wanted was sex, she could have gotten it. She could have convinced Marion that a good old-fashioned hatefuck was exactly what they needed to close the book on their interactions.

But no. She was being cautious. She was laying the groundwork because she wanted a solid foundation. She hugged herself and fought back the sudden urge to cry. There had been sex since Reggie died. She'd had other women in her bed and she'd never felt guilty. Now, however, for the first time she felt like she might be betraying the woman she swore to love before anyone else for the rest of her life. There was never a ceremony or a formal exchanging of vows, but the commitment was there. Now she was maybe considering something real, with someone else.

"Marion Vogt," she whispered. She shook her head at her foggy reflection in the glass and crossed her arms over her chest. Why did it have to be her? Marion was beautiful, sure. She was talented, successful, tough as nails. She liked to swim, which was a big plus. She had no idea what was going to come from their conversation on the app. Maybe nothing. She would be fine with that. At least then she would be able to move on with her life and forget she'd ever heard of the caterer.

But if she did send another message...

If Marion responded...

She thought about what would have happened if their roles were reversed. If Reggie had been safe at home and Sofia got in a wreck on the way home from work. She didn't know how Reggie would have reacted, but she knew what she would hope. She would want Reggie to be with someone who made her happy, who appreciated how wonderful and weird and sweet Reggie could be. She was crying now, and she let out a sob when she thought of Reggie being alone and lonely. Three full years by herself with no one to come home to? It broke her heart.

She brought her hand to her mouth and chewed the thumbnail. What did she want to happen? A date? Could they even share a space together without something going awry? And how good of a kisser was Marion when she wasn't being sucker punched by another pair of lips?

"I'm sorry, Reggie," Sofia whispered. "I'm sorry I wasted so much time."

She moved away the window and walked back to her bed. Marion Vogt. Unexpected, unlikely, but with definite potential. As she turned off the lights she considered the fact that maybe the unexpected was exactly what she needed.

CHAPTER FIFTEEN

MARION DIDN'T know how long she should expect to wait for another message from Sofia. A day? Two days, a week? She was at work the day after the initial exchange and noticed it was time for the Channel Six News to begin. She turned on the TV in her office and put it on KCTV. There she was, sitting at a desk next to the Ken Doll that served as her co-anchor, Del Stockton. She'd always thought of Del as an underwear model past his prime, pretty in a way that was clear he used to be even prettier. Sofia, however, was just full-stop gorgeous. She was wearing a teal dress under a black blazer.

"...fire tore through a Queen Anne warehouse this afternoon. Firefighter Kelly Lake who was at the scene said..."

Marion ignored the actual news story and looked into Sofia's eyes. The Back-Up segment was ostensibly about doing good in the world. She'd seen a few of them online and it was clear that her intentions were good. And she had to admit that if Beacon had been responsible for someone's guests getting food poisoning, she would have wanted someone to make them pay.

She watched the rest of the broadcast thinking of Sofia Kennedy as a neutral entity rather than her nemesis. She was charming and quick-witted, bantering with Del in between segments. When it was over and they segued into a game show,

Marion took out her phone and opened the MEOW app. She went to the inbox and stared at the last message she'd received from Sofia. She thought the implication was that Sofia would decide when to break the silence, but Marion was the wronged party. Sofia had reached out and it was up to Marion to either accept or decline.

"Saw you on the news tonight. You looked great. Didn't take down any innocent business-owners, either." She added a winking face to take some bite out of the comment. She put down the phone and went back to work, but the phone chimed before she could get back into what she'd been doing. She was surprised to see it was a notification from MEOW, a new Purr from S_Queen.

"Thank you. I try to keep my assassinations to a minimum these days. I must only use my powers for good."

"You have powers?" Marion sent back.

"Various spells and potions."

Marion surprised herself by laughing out loud. "Good to know you're not putting them towards evil deeds anymore. Did I make you see the error of your ways?"

"Yes, you're my savior."

"All in a day's work."

After a few minutes, Sofia responded, "I have to record a few things for the late broadcast. Will you be watching?"

"I may tune in."

"I'll try to sneak you a message."

Marion smiled. Sneak her a message? It was like high school, but she had to admit she was intrigued by the idea. "I'll keep an eye out."

She put the phone down, assuming the conversation was over. She went back to work on her laptop and glanced up as Courtney leaned into the room.

"Hey. I thought I heard laughing in here."

"I can laugh. It's my office. And my company. The only people not allowed to laugh are my downtrodden peons."

Courtney said, "Yes, ma'am. I'm going to head out."

"Okay. Who else is here?"

"Once I'm gone, it's just you, boss lady. Lisa's team is out at the engagement party."

Marion looked at her watch. "Wow. When did it get this late? Hold on a second and I'll walk out with you."

Courtney said, "Walk out with me, or do you want a ride home? I was going to grab dinner on my way home. You could join me."

"Hard to pass up that offer."

She closed her laptop and gathered her things. When she picked up her phone, Courtney gestured at it in a manner that was almost casual.

"So. MEOW app?"

"What?" Marion followed Courtney to the back door.

"I actually walked by the office door and saw you hunched over your phone. It has to be that app of yours, right? Someone with potential?"

"I don't know about potential. Potentially potential, maybe."

Courtney said, "Well, that's all you can hope for. Let me know if it progresses further."

"I will." She locked the back door. "Right now it's still very much in the development phase. Just talking online, no big deal. Nothing to get excited about. Now... where are you taking me for dinner?"

They had some fish tacos at the Tin Table, staying to share a dessert. Courtney tried to get more information about the woman she'd met on MEOW. "If you think I'm going to make fun of you, rest assured I completely support those apps. They're amazing once you get past the creeps and the weirdoes." Courtney furrowed her brow. "Do they have creeps and weirdo's on lesbian dating apps? I would think that's exclusively a straight male trait."

"We all have the potential to be creepy weirdo's," Marion said, "but I admit, straight men have perfected it."

When they finished their meal, Courtney drove Marion home. She arrived with more than enough time to catch the local news, so she busied herself on her laptop until eleven o'clock came. She tuned to Channel Six as the last prime-time show was ending. Del's voiceover teased the top stories before the image cut to the studio with the short burst of music that accompanied their opening graphics. News theme songs were always so triumphant, so joyful, considering some of the stories that followed it.

Sofia was wearing the same outfit as the early broadcast, and she began the news by reading a report of a traffic accident on Alaskan Way. She was completely professional, giving no indication she was planning some kind of message to a viewer. Marion laughed at herself for being so eager, but the curiosity would drive her nuts if she didn't watch.

After approximately ten minutes of reading the news, the music swelled to indicate a commercial break. "Coming up," Sofia said in a voiceover, "we've got Evan with the sports, but Reed will be the real MVP when you hear this weekend's forecast. Stay with us."

Marion smiled slowly. That had to be message, a wink at her MEOW username. She took out her phone and sent a reply. "The P is my middle name. MVP sounds better than MPV."

"What does it stand for?"

"Penelope."

The news came back from commercial just after she sent the message. As the camera moved in to show both anchors, Marion saw Sofia was looking down at the phone she was holding next to her hip, blocking the screen from Del. When the lights came up, she tapped the screen with her thumb and slipped the phone back into her pocket. She faced the camera with the same professional demeanor as before, but now the smile reached her eyes.

Marion laughed and shook her head. "Unbelievable. Sofia Kennedy." The woman she would have crossed the street to avoid just a week earlier. Now they were... what, flirting? Becoming friends? She watched the rest of the broadcast in case there were any further messages, but Sofia stuck to the script. She waited through the weather forecast, then the sports. Just before the news came back, she opened the MEOW app and sent a Purr.

"We should probably meet in person."

"We've met in person. Multiple times."

"I don't think so. I'd remember meeting this person."

Del said goodnight, Sofia told the audience to stay tuned for the late-night talk show coming up next, and the music played again. The lights dimmed, and Sofia fished her phone out of her pocket. If there were any lingering doubts about who she was conversing with, they had been eliminated. A few seconds after the talk show, started, a new Purr arrived.

"Are you sure? Considering how it's gone in the past?"

Marion sent back, "I'm sure. If we can't stand to be in the same room together, then all this is just wasting each other's time. Do you have a place you're comfortable going, since you're not out?"

"Do you know Sea/TT/Les?"

"Well enough to get myself there. Tomorrow night?"

Sofia said, "Nine o'clock?"

"I'll be there."

She switched to her browser and looked up the nightclub's address. It wasn't far from Pike Place, near a few other gay bars and dance clubs. She got up and went to her closet in search of something worthy of wearing to that part of town. There was a reason she preferred hooking up on the app. No loud music she had to pretend to like, no dressing up, no anxiety about people judging her while she was busy judging everyone around her. It was so much easier with the phone as a barrier between them. She could present herself as a full person instead of just that day's outfit and makeup.

Now she was doubly stressed out. She was not only meeting up with a potential... whatever... but it was Sofia Kennedy. A celebrity. A celebrity with whom she'd had a handful of adversarial encounters. The meet-up was supposed to be a clearing of the air and a clean slate, so what sort of wardrobe did that require? How sexy should she aim for? How conservative? Was it a business-like meeting? She chucked her red leather jacket as too provocative. The white turtleneck was a bit too 'soccer mom.'

She finally settled on her white blouse, a blue scarf, and her gray-knit beanie. It didn't come off as too seductive, but it definitely said that she was trying. She set out the clothes on the armchair next to the closet and stared down at them.

"Okay. Tomorrow night. We'll see what we see then."

She turned away from the outfit and went to take a shower, hoping to get her mind off what would happen the next day.

"Stupid!" Sofia hissed. Sea/TT/Les was her turf, her sanctuary. If Marion liked the place but decided she couldn't bear to be around Sofia, then it might become a place Sofia would have to avoid. But when she thought about it, there was a certain poetic justice to having the peace summit happen on her turf. Their first encounter had been on Marion's turf, at her office, a place she presumably felt safe. Then they met in the station lobby... neutral territory. The pool, Sofia's turf. The kitchen on Whidbey Island, Marion's. So now it was Sofia's turn.

She sent the last few messages from the news desk. Del and the other guys had wandered back to the newsroom and the lights had been dimmed. The cameras still ringed the area with their heads bowed like oddly-dressed monks worshipping at an altar. She could hear voices elsewhere in the building echoing down the dark corridors. The last broadcast of the day was over and the majority of people were heading home. They would have a skeleton crew just in case of breaking news that required a live report, but Sofia was one of the lucky few who got to escape to the comfort of home.

She pushed back and slipped her phone into her pocket. Normally she didn't have it on her during a broadcast, but she couldn't resist sneaking a few peeks during commercials. It was nice to know someone was out there watching, a pair of eyes on the other side of the lens. She hadn't really had that feeling since...

"Reggie," she said under her breath. Reggie used to watch all of her broadcasts when they first got together. She tapered off after a year or two ("I can only take so much of you telling me all the horrible things happening in the world," she said) but when she did watch, she would text cute comments during the breaks. Sort of like Marion had done with the app. If Reggie had been at home watching the news, then she wouldn't have been in the street when...

She stopped herself before she could go down that road. She walked down the corridor between the set and the newsroom, pausing to look out the windows. She loved the view but she had seen it so many times that she usually ignored it. There was always something else to occupy her attention. Copy for a news story, her cell phone, some other member of the news team talking to her. She crossed her arms. Another window, another view of Seattle, and Sofia alone behind the glass. It would be nice to have someone to share the views with again.

She supposed they would know soon enough if Marion was going to be that someone.

CHAPTER SIXTEEN

BONITA TRIED not to notice anyone who happened to be in Sea/TT/Les on any given night. Their patrons chose to drink there because of the privacy policy. No one could be recognized, no one could be called out, and no one had to hide their preferences. She'd seen football and baseball players, she'd seen movie and TV stars, she'd seen politicians and tech gurus all hooking up in the dim light between her position at the bar and the dance floor. She didn't even tell her girlfriend who she happened to see, no matter how many times she was asked.

But Bonita was only human. Now and again she would see someone who made her stop in her tracks and stare. An athlete famous for telling anyone who would listen how "the gays" were destroying the nation once got a hand job on the dance floor. The hypocrisy irritated her, but the bar's promise had to extend to everyone, otherwise it was useless.

She was working the bar when she spotted the sexy lady from the news walk in the door. Sofia Kennedy, like a real-life superhero, swooping in to save the day from some thief or con artist. She was even prettier in person. Her hair used to be long, but the past few years she'd kept it short. It was upswept now, almost but not quite a pompadour, leaving the elegant curve of her neck exposed above the collar of her purple blouse.

At first, Bonita thought she was on the prowl. The makeup, the buttons of her blouse undone far enough to reveal her cleavage, the way her eyes scanned the room from one corner to the other without pause. But on the second pass her eyes locked onto her prey, a woman in a white blouse and a tan jacket. She was wearing a gray beanie with blonde curls peeking out from underneath. The blonde had been nursing the same drink since she'd arrived. Bonita saw the glass was nearly empty and timed her approach so she would arrive at the same time as Sofia.

"Marion," Sofia said, and the blonde turned to greet her. They both smiled nervously, neither moving toward the other. No hug, no kiss on the cheek, not even an awkward handshake. Marion stepped to one side so Sofia could join her at the bar. Bonita approached and gestured at the empty glass between Marion's hands.

"Get you another?" Bonita asked.

"Uh, yeah. Sofia, do you want something?"

Sofia said, "Ah, amaretto."

Bonita nodded and refilled the glass for the blonde, Marion apparently, before mixing Sofia's drink. She was close enough that she could overhear their conversation.

"Is this awkward?" Marion said. "I want to get that out of the way first."

"Maybe a little. The alcohol will help."

"I'll let you know. I have a bit of a head start on you there."

Sofia said, "We'll see how it goes."

Bonita delivered their drinks and moved to help another customer. She had learned over the years how to read body language, which told her so much more than their actual words would have. Marion was tense, eager in a way but also very guarded about being near Sofia. Sofia's shoulders were set in a hard line and she kept her head up. When she took a drink of her amaretto, she did so in a way that kept her eyes on her companion. They were incredibly wary of each other but also hopeful about the meeting. Bonita poured another drink for a customer at the other end of the bar, got more bottles from the back, and kept checking on the couple whenever she got a spare moment.

When she refilled their glasses, both women had loosened up. Whether it was the alcohol or the conversation was anybody's guess. "~most days," Sofia was saying. "I might miss one or two mornings, but if I go more than three I start to get twitchy."

"I wish I had a pool I could use that frequently." Marion saw Bonita gesture at her glass and nodded. "Yes, please. As it is, I use swimming to treat myself."

"You have to have ways to treat yourself." Sofia retrieved the cherry from her glass before offering it up for a refill. She brought it to her mouth and let her lips close around it, her lipstick just a shade darker than the skin of the cherry. It was more of a kiss than a bite, and she kept her eyes on Marion as she performed the move. Marion caught the end of the move and, though she didn't react, definitely let her gaze linger on Sofia's mouth.

Bonita had to fight a smile as she handed back the freshened drinks. It might not happen tonight, it might not happen in the near future, but she'd seen enough flirting to know when a couple was going to end up in bed together. With the anchorwoman and the blonde in the beanie, there was no doubt in her mind that they were well on their way.

"What do you think about her?"

Sofia looked at the bartender, who Marion had indicated with a quick flip of her pinkie finger. She was petite but muscular, wearing a dark red vest that revealed the tattoos on her arms. She was Aussie, a redhead, and definitely attractive. "I think she would be a nice distraction for a night. Why? You looking to end this early and head home with a runner-up?"

Marion grinned. "No. I'm just trying to wrap my head around the fact you're gay. It would help if I could figure out what your type is."

"I don't have a type."

"That's what everyone says."

Sofia shrugged. "I could really fall for anyone. I have. Older than me, younger than me. Redhead, brunette. I've dated butch women, femmes, everything in between."

"Tell me about one of them."

Sofia considered Reggie, but she didn't want to use the pinnacle of her romantic life as a random example. "There was a woman I knew in college. Mal. She was my resident advisor, so she was a few years older than me. Blonde. Gorgeous. She smoked, which was usually a deal-breaker for me. But just a glimpse of those blue eyes and that devilish smile through a puff of smoke..." She laughed. "She looked like a dragon. God, she was sexy."

Marion smiled. "I met my first girlfriend in the foster system.

We were both placed in this house... beautiful home, great parents, but we were rebels for the sake of rebelling. We would run away, shoplift, basically act like hoodlums until our foster parents came and dragged us back home. One night we got all the way to Mount Vernon. Did you know they have tulips up there?"

"I did."

"She wanted to pluck one to give it to me, but I didn't want it to die. So instead we drew tulips on each other's wrists. She kissed mine when she was done drawing it." She took a deep breath and let it out slowly. "It was like a door opened. Like... yep, okay, didn't know I was questioning it, but it's crystal clear now." She chuckled and tucked a loose curl behind her ear. "We fooled around in an empty house we broke into. The dad of the foster family tracked us down somehow, dragged us home. The mother realized we were just trying to give them an excuse to abandon us. She refused to. She decided we needed discipline in our lives. Sara got to choose an instrument, and I ended up in the kitchen. It was the same thing that happened when Sara kissed my wrist. Like... 'okay, yeah, this is it.'"

Sofia said, "That's a beautiful story. Where is Sara now?"

"Violinist with the Washington State Orchestra."

"Seems like you both ended up doing pretty well for yourselves."

Marion shrugged and nodded at the same time.

During the story, their space at the bar had gotten progressively smaller. Marion suggested getting some breathing room outside and Sofia agreed. They settled their tab and headed out. Sofia led the way, taking advantage of the lull in their conversation to consider how things were going. She was embarrassed with herself for pulling the trick with the cherry. It was a cheap trick and something she ordinarily wouldn't have done, but the look in Marion's eye was worth it. Just because they were being civil to each other didn't mean she had to give up her victories.

They stepped outside and, after a brief debate, headed west toward the famous Public Market sign. Marion had a scarf that she wrapped loosely around her shoulders as they walked. They were shoulder to shoulder, neither of them leading the other, neither in a rush to continue the conversation. When they got closer to the market, Sofia suggested taking a detour by the gum wall.

Marion chuckled. "Ah, one of the most disgusting landmarks the world has to offer. Why not? I remember the city was going to clean this up. What happened there?"

Sofia said, "They did clean it. My friend Kathryn covered the power-washing. For the first time in twenty years, the walls of Post Alley were completely clean of gum. But in less than a week, the gum wall had made a triumphant return, the product of a flash mob who proved that you can never tell what people will be nostalgic for."

Marion laughed. "Wow. You got all 'reporter' on me just then."

Sofia mimed holding a microphone and touched her ear. "Back to you in the studio, Del."

Marion chuckled again and led Sofia down the sloped brick path to the alley. The first part of the alley was more of a tunnel, with a canopy created by the street covering their heads as they passed the gum wall. The air was sweet, a mixture of peppermint and spearmint that combined to smell oddly like doughnuts. Sofia felt the urge to take Marion's hand but knew it was far too soon for that. Instead she put her hands in her pockets and watched her feet as they passed the metal flowers rising from the sculpture garden. The air was chilly but there was no rain, no breezes. They passed a few people but no one gave Sofia a second look or whispered a comment to their companions about who she might be.

"So what's the verdict on tonight?" Marion finally asked.

"I think it went well. Is going well. Is it over?"

Marion shrugged. "I'm not sure what else we could do. But I did have fun."

"So did I. I enjoyed getting to know you." Marion nodded. "So I guess... maybe we should do it again. Dinner?"

"Is there anywhere you can go on a date without worrying about people seeing you?" Sofia started to answer, but Marion continued. "Why don't you just come over to my place? Around eight o'clock? I'll cook dinner."

Sofia said, "That sounds great."

"Any dietary restrictions?"

"No. Do your worst."

They compared schedules as they walked back toward the main road. They ended up outside the art museum with a plan to meet the following Thursday when Sofia wasn't going to be on the air and Marion didn't have an event to cater. They stood under the Hammering Man sculpture, both of them obviously waiting for the other to be the one to say a final goodbye and end their night together. Sofia had truly enjoyed their conversation at the bar and didn't want to look like she was eager to part ways.

"Why did you come after me?" Marion suddenly snapped.

Sofia was startled. "Wh-what?"

"I've had a great time with you tonight. I'm looking forward to cooking dinner for you next week. But this can't go any further until I know why you came after me so hard."

"Oh." Sofia looked toward the road.

"Come on. We shared the good stuff. But a friend of mine recently told me that the bad stuff is just as important to get out of the way. You and I have been digging through the bad stuff almost exclusively, so this is the last thing that could stand in the way of something that might be truly special. At least I think it might be."

Sofia said, "I think it might be, too." Her voice was meek and small. "Okay. The first time we met, when I ambushed you outside of your building. You fought back by mentioning the night I froze on-air."

Marion furrowed her brow. "That? I can't possibly be the first person to make fun of you for that. Nick Young had a whole running gag about it on *Settle In, Seattle!* for a few months."

"It's not that," Sofia said. "It was... after you brought it up, you said that I was unprofessional because I'd been thrown by 'some idiot woman.'"

Marion flinched. "Oh, God. I said that? What an awful thing to say. Obviously it's a good thing that you still have empathy after all these years of reporting horrible news night after night..."

"She was my girlfriend."

"She..."

"The woman who died. I froze because I recognized her bicycle on the live feed."

Marion covered her mouth with one hand, her eyes widening. "No."

"So that's why I came after you so hard. It wasn't your fault..."

"Not my fault?" Marion said. "Not... oh, God. Forget the tissues. You should have thrown the receptionist's phone at me."

Sofia chuckled and a tear slipped out of the corner of her eye. "You couldn't have known."

"Still, it was a shitty thing to say. Even if you didn't know her, it's still someone who died. God, I must have been really pissed off at you to say that." She shook her head in disgust. "I would have declared war, too. What was her name?"

"Reggie. Regina."

Marion said, "That's why you chose the name 'queen' for your MEOW profile."

Sofia looked surprised, but after a moment she nodded slowly.

"I don't think 'sorry' really covers what I did, but I apologize from the bottom of my heart."

"I forgive you," Sofia said. Saying it felt better than she would have thought, so she faced Marion fully and met her eye. "I forgive you. And I'm sure Reggie would have forgiven you ages ago. You were just defending yourself against someone who had ambushed you with a camera shoved in your face. I shouldn't have gotten so mad just because you fought back."

Marion said, "It was still a low blow."

"It was."

Marion reached out and used the back of her index finger to wipe the tear off Sofia's cheek. Sofia closed her eyes. Above them, the Hammering Man continued to raise and drop his steel hammer in a never-ending arc.

"Sofia?"

"Hm?"

"I don't know how to get home from here."

Sofia laughed and opened her eyes. She turned and looked down the street, hoping for a bus stop or a miraculous cab with its on-duty light shining. She fished her phone out of her pocket.

"I'll call you an Uber."

Marion nodded and put her hands in her pockets as Sofia summoned a chariot for her.

CHAPTER SEVENTEEN

THE REST of the week, Sofia was plagued by bad dreams and unwelcome memories of Reggie. Their life together hadn't been all sunshine and roses; nobody's was. Reggie could be immature and Sofia could be selfish. Reggie held grudges and could rage like she was being paid for it. Sofia was a big fan of the silent treatment. She would skip calls or texts just to prove a point, a practice she now felt horrible about. When she thought of all the missed conversations or just a simple "see you soon," she regretted every time she had put the phone down without responding.

The dreams weren't actual memories. She saw Reggie throwing clothes around the living room, heard her hollering from the other room but couldn't find her when she went looking. In the morning, sitting in the sauna after a punishing swim, she realized that the rage demon in her dreams wasn't Reggie at all, but her own guilt at her burgeoning feelings for Marion. Reggie wasn't perfect, but jealousy was not one of her faults. She would casually point out women she found attractive when they were out in public. She would Netflix movies with actresses she knew Sofia found sexy and Sofia would do the same in return.

"Commitment doesn't mean sexual attraction is turned off," Reggie said. "We're still human beings and we both obviously have excellent taste in women. So why feel guilty about looking?"

A woman came into the sauna and took a seat cater-corner to where Sofia was. The woman looked prim and proper; head held high and shoulders back even when she was wearing a towel. Her dark hair was piled on top of her head. She positioned her feet on the step below her, leaned back against the wall, and closed her eyes. Sofia watched her and knew that if Reggie had been there, she would have commented on the woman's legs, her breasts, the way her tongue peeked out to moisten her lips.

"Some people may have a problem with how you gawk at them," Sofia warned.

Reggie said, "If they do, I'll apologize."

"You're a predator."

"I'm a devotee of the female form. I'd never do anything with them. And they're welcome to look at me in return."

"Quite an ego you've got there."

Reggie would laugh and drape herself against Sofia's side. "I can't help it. My partner boosts my self-esteem so high, I think I'm a goddess."

The woman opened her eyes and saw Sofia staring at her. She smiled and brushed her hand over her thigh, just under the hem of her towel. It was casual enough to be an innocent move, but paired with the unblinking stare, Sofia knew there was an extra invitation to the gesture. She smiled, shook her head once, and looked away.

"Oh my god, she wants you." She urged her inner Reggie voice to shut up. "Go over there. Go down on her. I'll watch." She closed her eyes and tried to think of song lyrics to drown out the voice. "I bet she would be a firecracker."

Sofia had to retreat. She pushed away from the wall and stood up. "Would you like me to adjust the temperature?" she asked, hoping the other woman wouldn't feel guilty for running her off.

"No, it feels great."

Sofia nodded and left the sauna. She showered, dressed for work, and left the gym. Despite her subconscious attempts to sabotage herself, she was actually incredibly excited about her date with Marion. She knew there was a thin line between hate and love, that passion could be both positive and negative, but usually it went the other way. Love faded and became disinterest or it became something she took for granted. She couldn't remember ever feeling such rage and animosity for someone she ended up actually caring for.

There was truth in what Marion had said, or what Marion's

friend had said. Everyone got the good stuff out of the way first. Their likes and dislikes, the things that would make them an appealing partner. She and Marion had taken care of all the bad elements right away. If they could get past that, if they could find common ground after considering each other an enemy, there was a chance they could make something that lasted.

She drummed her thumbs on the steering wheel to the beat of the Vienna Teng song playing on her iPod as she drove, trying not to overthink about what was going to happen Thursday.

The Bower/Maurice wedding was held at Storybook Farm, a gorgeous rustic farmhouse about an hour outside of Seattle. The owners of the farm had a list of approved caterers their clients could choose from, and through Courtney's networking and a slew of phone calls, Beacon had recently been added to the list. The wedding was their first job at the venue, so she wanted to be on-hand to make sure everything went smoothly for what she considered to be their audition. If Storybook was happy with them, it could mean a huge uptick in business. Storybook's only stipulation was that they preferred a color other than black for their uniforms, so Marion had her team outfitted in white dress shirts under gold vests.

Marion kept her head on work, but another part of her mind was set aside to worry over what she was going to cook for Sofia. She still felt as if their relationship was in a trial period. An awkward step or a misguided comment could throw them back to where they had started. She didn't want that to happen. She felt like there was real potential for something great between them. She just had to be sure to watch her mouth and not inadvertently insult anyone else precious to Sofia.

The reception would take place in the big red barn near the main house. Her team had set everything up and now they only had to wait for the ceremony to end. Marion snuck around the edge of the barn to take a peek and saw the two women standing in front of the officiant. The brunette wore a white tuxedo with a gold cummerbund, the blonde wore a dark blue suit. Marion smiled as she watched them exchange vows she was too far away to hear. When she started working at Beacon, every wedding they were hired for was straight. As she rose through the ranks, more and more gay and lesbian couples started hiring them. Now she estimated they did a majority of lesbian weddings, with straight and gay couples making up an equal part of the other half. She didn't know what drew the ladies to Beacon, but if she ever found out she would definitely double down on it.

The brides kissed and Marion found herself applauding with the rest of the guests. She'd never thought of herself in that position, in front of her friends and loved ones dedicating her life to someone else. Weddings were for other people, people who knew how to exist in a family unit. She was more than content behind the scenes making sure everyone else was well-fed and taken care of. But all of that didn't mean she was unable to appreciate the sentiment.

The happy couple moved down the aisle, which was Marion's cue to get the ball rolling on the food. She left her peeping spot and went to send out the troops. The first course was a choice between soup or salad, and they had the Caesar salads and chanterelle soups ready to go. The second course was cedar-planked salmon and, while her crew was heading out the door with their plates and bowls, she moved to make sure the fish was ready to move out.

At the back of the room was the crowning piece of the reception: the cake. Beacon hadn't been responsible for making it but they would be the ones bringing it out to the main room. It was a simple but gorgeous cake with a navy ribbon around each layer. The base had a wispy blue feather made of fondant attached to a blue frosting rose. The cake was topped by two cartoon people: a blonde woman wearing scrubs and a brunette in a paramedic's uniform. It didn't take much imagination to figure out how they had met, and she silently wished the couple luck as she passed their cake.

By the time the couple danced their dance and headed off to a life of wedded bliss, Marion was ready to chop her feet off at the ankles and declare both her legs DOA. She was exhausted from the constant movement from one section of the barn to the other, checking on dishes and putting out potential fires with waiters and guests, making sure the entire thing went as smoothly as possible so the venue wouldn't take them off the list of approved vendors. At the end of the night she wondered if it was worth the hassle, but she remembered the check and decided she could tough it out.

When she got home, she took a long bath to work out the kinks in her legs and back. She brought her iPad with her so she could look up recipes for her date with Sofia. She had a whole catalogue of personal favorites, the meals she could cook with one hand tied behind her back, but the question was which one would be best for Sofia? Too many people thought food was just something to shove in their faces, something interchangeable. Food was like clothing; everyone had a style whether they knew it or not. She had to find the right thing for Sofia and pair that with the tone she hoped to set for the evening.

Of course that meant she had to decide what tone she wanted. Did she plan on going to bed with Sofia when the meal was over? Did she want to angle the night toward more romantic or stay solidly on neutral ground to let Sofia make the decision. She scrolled through her recipe lists, pausing on one before moving on to the next, skipping back three and then dismissing four right out of hand. Steak was an iffy prospect. She could see Sofia eating steak, but it also didn't seem like her first choice. Lamb or veal was also a bit too far off the mark.

As a chef in Seattle, she tended to lean toward fish. But not salmon. Sofia would be disappointed by salmon whether she realized it or not. Something a bit more unexpected. Fillet of sole. She could do something with sole in white wine, maybe garnished with lemon. She had most of what she needed in the kitchen and she could pick up the fish at the market in the morning.

When she got out of the bath she opened the MEOW app on her phone and sent a Purr to Sofia. "I think I have tomorrow night's menu sorted. Preferences on salad? Dressing? Last chance to declare any allergies."

She had dressed for bed by the time Sofia responded. "No allergies, Caesar for the salad, and what wine can I bring?"

"White," Marion sent back, then paused and added a second message. "It's weird we're still using the app to communicate. You can call or text me." She put her number at the end of the message. A few minutes the phone chimed.

"Now you have my number. Use it wisely."

Marion smiled.

She went into the kitchen in her pajamas and made sure she really did have everything she needed. She had enough wine for cooking, and she lined up the salt and pepper next to the stove like soldiers awaiting their orders. She had flour, eggs, lemons, but she needed a green onion, mushrooms, and whipping cream. She made a list for the market and turned out the lights on her way to bed. Fillet of sole liked to be served immediately, so she was going to make its preparation part of the date. One of her exes called it culinary seduction and ever since she found ways to make sure her dates got a glimpse of her talents in the kitchen.

She was eager to see if Sofia would be susceptible to her skills.

Chapter Eighteen

Sofia bought a bottle of 2007 Riesling from San Juan Vineyards. It had taken her less time to choose the bottle than it had to get ready. Everything she put on made her feel like she was getting ready for a broadcast. A blazer was far too professional. She had a few dresses that she felt were a bit too provocative for what the date was supposed to be. Although she wasn't entirely sure what it was supposed to be. Even her mental construct of Reggie refused to help her ("Sorry, babe, I'm all for moving on, but I'm not going to give you tips on how to dress for another woman. Good luck.").

She finally decided on a low-cut white blouse and a black skirt under a high-collared black jacket. It struck a nice middle ground between what she would wear to work and an outfit for one of the many events she had to attend as a local "celebrity." She arrived at Marion's wonderfully fragrant building a few minutes early, and it wasn't until she was standing directly in front of the apartment that she realized the smell was coming from within. She rang the bell and looked down at her outfit, rethinking it one last time before the door opened.

Marion looked phenomenal. Her blouse was a dark maroon and her jeans were black. Her hair was pinned back loosely enough that a few strands hung down around her face. For a moment Sofia thought it was a waste to not take her out in public and show off how good she looked, but then she caught another whiff of what was cooking and realized missing the meal would be the bigger loss. She managed a smile and held up the bottle.

"Hi. I brought the wine."

"Fantastic," Marion said as she took the bottle. "Come in. You look amazing."

Sofia said, "So do you. Whatever you're cooking smells wonderful."

Marion closed the door as Sofia scanned the room. The living room and kitchen were separated by a bar, creating a mostly open feeling. Marion took the wine into the kitchen and Sofia followed her. Despite the strong smells of a finished meal, the fish was sitting on the oven in a baking pan. Marion quickly washed her hands under the faucet and went back to a large salad bowl sitting next to the counter. She stuck both hands into the leaves and began mixing it with her fingers instead of utensils.

"Is that how you do it at Beacon?" Sofia asked.

Marion smiled and shook her head. "If we did, they'd wear gloves. But no, the size of the portions we make there, it just makes sense to be as careful as possible there. We don't want to end up on the news again." She grinned and looked sideways at Sofia, who accepted the jab with a slight nod of her head. "When I'm at home, I like getting in there and really feeling the food. Don't worry, I frequently wash my hands. I'm a food nut, but I'm smart."

Sofia said, "Good to know." She could smell fish and lemon in the air, both of which made her water at the mouth as she leaned against the counter. "So how can I smell the finished product if the uncooked fish is sitting right there?"

Marion smiled sheepishly. "I may have cooked a test meal about an hour ago, just to make sure everything went well. It did, so I gave it to my neighbors."

"Wow, I want to live next door to you. What can I do to help?"

"Ah, slice up these lemons? Super-thin. The knives are over there."

Sofia moved the lemons onto the chopping block and retrieved a knife. As she sliced, she watched Marion pour a small amount of salt and pepper into her hand. She held it over the fish and carefully sprinkled the combination onto the fillets. Sofia paused slicing and focused on the way Marion's fingers moved. Long and slender fingers, the nails trimmed short and unpolished, still managed to look elegant as she brushed the excess spice over the sink and washed her hands again. Sofia finished slicing and stepped back so Marion could see.

"Good? Or thinner?"

"That should be perfect. Could you open the wine? The opener is near the knives."

Sofia retrieved the bottle as Marion put the lemon slices on the fish. She found the opener and cut away the foil. When she had the bottle open, she scanned the immediate area before she asked, "And the glasses..."

She turned and saw Marion was standing right behind her. She had just enough time to be startled before Marion cupped her face with wet hands and leaned in to kiss her. Sofia made a sound of surprise, one hand automatically landing on Marion's hip while the other went to her shoulder. She turned her head so their lips would line up more naturally and Marion rewarded her with a flicker of tongue. Sofia stepped away from the counter and pressed her hip against Marion's. Marion broke the kiss as suddenly as she'd started it. Sofia dropped one hand and put the other to her mouth, staring in wide-eyed curiosity.

"Now we're even," Marion said, averting her gaze as if suddenly shy.

"What?"

"The kiss. At the party I catered..."

"Oh!" Sofia chuckled, heat rising in her cheeks. "Yeah, I suppose we are."

Marion took the wine bottle from her and took to the over. She poured it over the fish and then placed the tray into the oven. She twisted the knob and turned to face Sofia.

"So, now we have twenty minutes to kill."

Sofia crossed the kitchen. Marion stood up straighter in anticipation, putting her hands on Sofia's hips as she pressed against her. They kissed again, their first mutually-instigated kiss. Sofia wrapped her arms around Marion, one at the shoulder and another around her waist, and turned Marion away from the heat of the oven. Sofia teased with her tongue but Marion wouldn't grant any ground. She turned her head and moved her lips to Sofia's neck, kissing from her jaw down to the high collar of her jacket. Sofia grunted and curled her hands in fistfuls of Marion's shirt.

"Marion..."

"Miss Vogt," Marion whispered.

Sofia's lips curled into a smile. "Really?"

"Say it."

"Whatever you want, Miss Vogt."

Marion moaned and swept her tongue over Sofia's throat, making her eyelids flutter. She was feeling weak in the knees and leaned against Marion for support, leaning back until Marion's lips were available to her. They kissed again, and this time Marion let Sofia do whatever she wanted. She thrust with her tongue and nipped at Marion's bottom lip, one hand stroking Marion's back while the other moved up into her hair.

"The whipping cream..." Marion twisted at the waist and scanned the counter. She pulled away from Sofia and grabbed the small white bowl that Sofia had overlooked. She moved it closer, dipped two fingers into the frothy contents, and then straightened back up. She dabbed the white cream on Sofia's neck and leaned in to thoroughly lick it off. Sofia grunted again and pressed Marion against the counter.

"I don't want dinner to burn..."

"We still have... like... fifteen minutes."

Sofia leaned back and looked into Marion's eyes.

"Oh. Right..."

She extricated herself as carefully as she could and they retreated to their separate corners. Sofia adjusted her jacket while Marion straightened her blouse.

Marion cleared her throat. "Uh, music... there's music. In the living room. Stereo. The stereo is in the living room and... it makes music..."

Sofia grinned. "I'll go see if I can figure it out."

She went into the living room and found the stereo. As she was going through the CDs next to the machine, Marion called out, "I also have an iPod with speakers if you'd prefer. I do occasionally visit the twenty-first century."

Sofia chuckled. She'd found a Radiation Canary album and put it in the slot. She advanced it to the third track, her personal favorite, and then turned on the shuffle. The music filled the apartment, Lana Kent's magnificent voice rising above the violin. *"So put your head against the window, we'll be there before you know. Trust me to get you there. Tonight you're my passenger."* She went back to the kitchen where Marion was taking a drink from her wine. She'd poured a glass for Sofia as well, and she retrieved it and lifted a silent toast to Marion before taking a sip.

"So... another twelve minutes or so. I suppose we should fill the time somehow."

Marion smiled against the rim of her glass and kept her mouth shut.

"So you cook with your hands a lot?"

Marion shrugged. "From time to time. Making crusts or dumplings, it's almost a necessity. It feels weird to use a tool for those things. But if I'm sprinkling shredded cheese or salt or seasoning, the hand is the best way to do it." She almost added her typical comment about being extremely talented with her fingers, but she was still trying to quell the sparks ignited by their earlier kiss. They had finished dinner and moved on to after-dinner drinks, but she still had no idea what the next step was going to be. She could tell from the way Sofia was nursing her drink that she wasn't sure, either. They both wanted the night to continue, she was sure, but neither of them was willing to take the step and say it out loud.

"I think it's a nice touch," Sofia said. "It makes it more... intimate, I guess. Made by hand."

Marion smiled. "I wish I'd had you bring some dessert. I have some Ben & Jerry's, but I'm saving that for about two weeks from now."

"What happens in two weeks?"

Marion raised an eyebrow.

"Oh, right. The unwanted visitor. Always good to have some ice cream on hand for that." Sofia smiled. "Isn't there a place near here that lets you build your own ice cream sandwiches?"

"Oh! Yes, there is. If we hurry they might even still be open."

"What are we waiting for? Let's go!"

It was close to ten-thirty by the time they got to the ice cream truck, but the owners were more than happy to fill one final order. Sofia got brown sugar cookies with mint chocolate chip filling, while Marion chose chocolate chip cookies and coffee ice cream filling. The interior lights of the cart switched off as they walked away with their treats in-hand.

"Coffee ice cream? This late at night?" Sofia asked.

Marion didn't know how to take that. Was Sofia teasing her, or did she really not intend for it to be a late night? She shrugged and said, "It's never too late for coffee anything."

"That is true, I suppose." She looked ahead, west toward the harbor. "It's a gorgeous night. Do you want to go straight back to your place or should we walk for a while?"

"We should at least walk until we finish our ice cream."

"Sounds like a solid plan."

They walked to the corner in silence, eating their treats and watching the occasional car pass. They were waiting to cross the street when someone coming from the opposite direction stopped, backed up, and twisted his neck to look at Sofia.

"Oh, shit, you're that Latina chick from Channel Six."

Marion immediately took a step to the right. She and Sofia hadn't been walking particularly close together, but she was suddenly very aware of her body language.

"Sofia Kennedy," Sofia said with a smile that told Marion she was just going to let the racist comment slide. "How are you this evening?"

"Good, good! Oh, man, can I get a picture? My man Dave, he loves you. He'd lose his shit if he was here right now."

"Sure, absolutely."

Marion had retreated to the wall as Sofia posed next to the man. He held his phone out with one hand, leaning in so his face was lined up with Sofia's. She smiled a big phony smile, and Marion suddenly realized she could tell the difference between a real smile and one put on for the public. More importantly, she hadn't seen a fake smile all evening, which meant...

Sofia thanked the man for watching and he continued on his way. Marion returned to Sofia's side and they crossed the street together.

"Sorry about that," Sofia said.

"Don't be. You have an adoring public to contend with. I understand."

"God, 'that Latina chick.' I've been doing this for over a decade and I'm still 'that Latina chick.'" She shook her head. "Two-time award winner for Back-Up. The woman who got an assisted living center to bring itself up to code. No, no. The Latina chick."

Marion didn't know how to respond to that, so she kept quiet. She reached out and brushed her hand against the sleeve of Sofia's coat before dropping it back to her side.

Sofia smiled weakly. "Thank you."

They walked for nearly an hour, much longer than they had to but long enough for Sofia to overcome her frustration and rediscover the joy of the night. When they got back to Marion's building, Sofia mentioned she had left her purse in Marion's apartment so they went up to get it. Marion let them in and turned on the lights.

"It's funny," she said, "I don't remember you having a purse when you showed up."

"I didn't."

Marion pushed the door shut just before Sofia kissed her. She let herself be pushed against the wall and hooked her leg on Sofia's hip. Sofia slid her hand along the underside of Marion's thigh and pushed her tongue into Marion's mouth, not waiting for an invitation this time. Marion didn't mind; her hands were already exploring the placket of Sofia's blouse in search of how to undo the buttons. After an entire night of uncertainty and mixed signals, she was more than ready to go. Sofia cupped her breast before following the curve of Marion's body to her waist.

"What do you want, Miss Vogt?"

Marion said, "I want you to fuck me, queenie."

Sofia smiled and bowed her head to kiss Marion's chest through her shirt. Marion kissed the top of Sofia's head, smelling her hair as she tried again to get the buttons of Sofia's blouse undone. She was feeling starbursts of warmth throughout her upper body from being kissed through her clothes, so she could only imagine what Sofia's lips would feel like on her skin.

"Let's get away from the door," Marion whispered. "People might wander by, even at midnight."

Sofia backed up a step, kissed Marion's breast through her shirt, and then suddenly recoiled. She straightened, stared at Marion, and did a quick scan of the apartment.

"What time is it?" she asked when she couldn't find a clock.

"What..." Marion nodded at the clock. "Eleven forty-seven. What, do you have a curfew? Fairy godmother gonna turn you back into a pumpkin at midnight?"

Sofia muttered under her breath. "Shit. Oh, no... no, no... I have to go."

"You have to what?"

Sofia checked her blouse, hands trembling. "I have to go. I'm sorry."

Marion said, "What the hell just happened?"

"I can't do this. I'm sorry, Marion, I just... I can't..."

Marion watched in complete confusion as Sofia brushed past her and fled the apartment. She pushed the hair out of her face, her cheeks and ears still burning as her body shrieked to find out why all the nice things that had been happening were suddenly not happening anymore. After a moment she stepped forward and slammed the door that Sofia had been in too much of a hurry to close behind her.

Sofia didn't turn on the lights as she walked into her apartment at twelve thirty-four. "I'm sorry," she whispered. "I'm so sorry. The twenty-second. Today is the twenty-second." She hadn't realized because the date was on the twenty-first. But if it had gone over into the next day, if she'd started the day in someone else's bed, she never would have forgiven herself. She felt queasy and clutched her stomach as she made her way to the bathroom. She didn't want to throw up Marion's meal, one of the best meals she'd ever had in her entire life, but her stomach wasn't feeling sentimental. She knelt in front of the toilet and threw up everything, muttering apologies to Marion in between her gasps for air.

When she was able to stand up, she went into the bedroom and took off the nice clothes she had put on for the date. She took off the fancy underwear she'd put on, just in case, and changed into a plain set. She put on a T-shirt and crawled under the blankets, tears wet on her face, stomach still knotted and tight from being sick. She hugged her pillow and closed her eyes, crying silently against the pillowcase.

"Happy birthday, Reggie," she whispered. "I'm so sorry. Happy birthday, baby."

Chapter Nineteen

THE NEXT morning, Courtney smirked as she leaned into Marion's office. "Hey! How was the big date last night?" Marion glared at her over the top of her laptop. Marion's smile faded and she stepped into the office. "Holy shit, that bad?"

Marion sighed and let her shoulders sag. "No. I don't know. It was going fantastic for a while." Courtney came into the office and sat across from Marion. "We had a great dinner. We made out for a little while. We went to get ice cream. We made out some more."

"Sounds good so far."

"And then she just slammed on the brakes and walked out."

"In the middle of...?"

Marion said, "Well, not in the middle. But we were heading up the on-ramp and she jumped out of the car just before we hit the highway."

"Ouch. No explanation?"

"None. She just freaked out because it was almost midnight and then vanished."

Courtney said, "But it was good up to that point?"

Marion exhaled sharply. "It was better than good. It was one of the best dates I've ever been on. She's amazing. She's brilliant and sexy and funny. But she's also the sort of person who flips out at the smallest provocation. I've sent her three texts already today trying to get an explanation, but she's ignored all of them. I'm starting to think she's not worth the headache."

"I'm sorry."

"Well, it happens." She sat up straighter and rolled her shoulders. "Is everything set for this weekend's events? What do we have?"

Courtney took out her phone and scrolled through the calendar. "We have the Perez anniversary, the Women's House fundraiser, and the advertising awards show. Which one do you want to take?"

"Women's House," Marion said. "Tyrone can do the advertising thing. He loves commercials."

Courtney grinned. "Then I'll do the Perezes. I love anniversaries. It's their sixtieth."

"Damn," Marion said. "Every year it gets less likely I'll ever have a sixtieth anniversary. That would just depress me."

"You'll get there. You and your lady will be the sexiest ninety-whatever-year-olds the world has ever seen."

Marion scoffed. "Me and my seven cats."

"Is that an old lady stereotype or a lesbian stereotype?"

"Little of both."

Courtney stood up. "I'll start working on the menus. Lunch?"

Marion checked the time. "Sure. Your choice."

When Courtney was gone, Marion took out her phone and checked for any missed messages. She wanted to be reasonable about Sofia's silence. Something had obviously rattled her and it made sense she might need a little time to work through it. But couldn't Sofia just *say* that? Respond to one of the texts and ask for a few hours to herself. It was common courtesy and Marion would be more than happy to grant her a little time if she would just show a sign of life. The longer the silence stretched on, the less reasonable she was likely to be when - or if - Sofia resurfaced.

She put her phone away and put Sofia out of her mind.

Sofia woke up the next morning and called in sick to work. Kathryn might get called to fill in for her at the desk, which would give her some much-needed airtime. She showered and put on sweats, put the laptop on the kitchen counter, and clicked on a "For You" video at random. Reggie's voice kept her company as she made coffee. Reggie had always reacted to her birthday like a kid. Up with the sun, special breakfast of all her favorites, and then a party on the closest weekend night. One year she hired a clown, another year she and Sofia spent the night in an arcade. Any frustration Sofia might've felt at the elaborate celebrations were smothered by how happy it made her to make Reggie happy. Now it pained her to know she'd only gotten to share five of Reggie's birthdays with her.

This year, her depression was deepened by what happened with Marion. She felt she'd done the right thing by leaving. If they'd ended up in bed together on Reggie's birthday, their first time would always be darkened by the date. But she also felt she'd irreparably damaged whatever good will she might have forged with Marion by leaving so abruptly. It really had been an amazing evening. Marion was so bright and clever, so talented in the kitchen, and Sofia just felt utterly comfortable in her presence. Marion had seen Sofia at her worst and was still willing to give her a chance. What were the odds of finding someone else who fit that description?

She picked up her phone and saw four texts waiting to be read. The first, "Is everything okay?", was the opening she needed to salvage the night. But the following texts were increasingly aggravated.

"Where are you?"

"What's going on?"

"Call me."

She put the phone on silent and placed it screen-down on the table. She covered her face with both hands. Reggie's video was still playing, her voice carrying through the speakers from four or five years ago unaware of Sofia's current predicament. She wanted to move on. The night before, halfway to being undressed with Marion Vogt, she'd definitely been ready. She pulled her hands down her face and looked at the laptop screen. Reggie was posing in front of a building Sofia didn't recognize, baseball cap pulled low over her face as she made Blue Steel expressions into the lens.

"Happy birthday, Reggie. The first year without you, I went whale-watching. The second year I bought a hundred dollars' worth of tokens and gave them to the kids having a birthday at the arcade. So for the third year without you, I thought I'd celebrate by fucking someone else."

She stood up and shut the laptop, grabbed her jacket on the way out the door, and walked out the door without her phone. She walked past the entrance to the garage and continued out to the street, walking first toward the gym but changing her mind halfway. She didn't have her access card for the pool and there was little reason to go otherwise. Instead she went north and west until she reached Alaskan Way to the Olympic Sculpture Park.

It was brighter than the day she'd met Reggie. Not a cloud in the sky and later in the morning. There were more people around as well, but she was able to get the bench where she was sitting when Reggie strolled into her life. She looked out over the harbor and let the constant roar of traffic block out the world around her. She watched the people who passed by, hoping one of them might be a ghost in a tuxedo who had come to offer advice. Sadly, no specters showed up to sit beside her.

"Okay, Reg," she whispered. "I need to know what to do. I need to know if it's okay to let you go just a little bit, because if I wait until tomorrow, I know I'm going to lose her. But if I chase her down on your birthday, I'm betraying you. I can't... I can't build a foundation with someone else. Not today of all days. You loved your birthday so much, and I can't bear to feel guilty whenever it rolls around." She blinked back tears. "Just tell me what to do, Reggie."

No answer came.

"What if this is the story I tell our grandkids?" Sofia whispered, remembering the way Reggie had kept her from walking away all those years ago. She closed her eyes and rolled her head back on her shoulders. Reggie would be able to turn it into a great story. 'The woman I loved finally moved on after I was gone. She found someone who was willing to take her shit but she almost screwed it up. So on my birthday, I gave *her* a gift.'

Sofia opened her eyes. "Reggie..." She chuckled under her breath. Reggie's birthday celebrations, as extravagant as they could get, were rarely about Reggie getting gifts. She rewarded others. She gave away tokens and reward tickets. She took pictures for other people so they would have mementos, since she couldn't have her own pictures with Sofia. The people she loved, the strangers around her. Reggie's gift was seeing other people happy.

"You would. You most definitely would."

She reached for her phone and realized she'd left it at home. She cursed under her breath and got up, using the long walk back to her apartment to figure out what she was going to say when she called Marion. An apology, of course, would be first and foremost. Then an invitation to dinner, something expensive and fancy to make up for the dinner Sofia had ruined. And then... well, and then, it would depend on if Marion was willing to pick things up where they left off.

Sofia let herself into her apartment and scooped up the phone. She turned it around and saw another message had arrived while she was gone.

"Don't bother. We gave it a shot."

"No," Sofia muttered. "No, no. God, please, no..." She dropped onto the couch and stared at the message, trying to think of a way she could pull it back. She kept her thumbs poised over the keypad, but no response presented itself to her.

Marion left work early, not long after Courtney headed out with a crew to cater a dance school graduation. She had finished the menus and didn't see much need to stick around the office. She could stare at the walls just as easily at home. Marion checked the MEOW app on the trolley ride home. Penny from Bothell messaged her again. "Full moon tonight. Wanna see how wild I can really get?" Marion was sorely tempted to agree, to jump off at the next stop and call an Uber to take her to Bothell so she could get fucked. It would help her recover from what Sofia had done to her the night before, and Penny was truly amazing in bed. But something stopped her from agreeing. It wasn't a case of infidelity, since she was ninety percent sure nothing would happen with Sofia, but it was too close to their near-perfect date for her to feel comfortable going to bed with someone else.

She sent Penny her regrets and pocketed her phone until they reached her stop. She got off the trolley and walked the rest of the way home. She rounded the corner of the hallway and slowed when she saw Sofia seated across from her apartment door. Sofia looked up and started to stand, so Marion moved faster to unlock her door and get inside as quickly as possible.

"Marion, please..."

"I don't want to hear it," Marion said, her back to Sofia. "Maybe I would have listened this morning, but it's too late. I tried. I reached out to you and you ignored me."

"I had a lot of thinking to do. Can we please–"

She had started to follow Marion inside. "No, I didn't invite you in." Sofia backed up a step. "I didn't expect a full explanation in a text. But you could have given me something. You chose not to."

"It's her birthday," Sofia said. "At twelve midnight, it would have been Reggie's birthday. I've never been with anyone on her birthday before. Her birthday, our anniversary, days that were special to us, those are... they're like holidays. I couldn't do what we were about to do on Reggie's birthday."

"Right," Marion said softly, eyes locked on the carpet next to Sofia's boots. "Right, I get that."

Sofia sighed with relief. "You do?"

"Of course I do. She's only been gone three years."

"I'm so glad to hear you say that. I went ahead and made reservations for~"

"I'm not going anywhere with you," Marion said.

Sofia blinked. "But you said you understood."

"I do. I understand everything. You attacked me because I inadvertently said something bad about her. You went after my business. And then you scuttled that whole magnificent night because it bumped up against her day. Reggie was the love of your life, but she's a field of landmines for me. I spent all day wondering what tripwire I'd triggered. Did you have fish with Reggie on your fourth date? Was the Radiation Canary song the first one you danced to? And what will be the next wrong step? I can't, Sofia. I can't keep tiptoeing around her. If we were meant to be, then..."

"But I think we are," Sofia said. "I think there's a chance we are."

Marion shrugged. "And I think it would hurt too much to prove you wrong. I'm sorry."

She shut the door and leaned her forehead against it. She knew that if Sofia knocked, she would open the door. She waited thirty seconds, then a full minute before she lifted her head and looked out the peephole. The corridor was empty, and Marion tried to convince herself she was happy about that.

CHAPTER TWENTY

SOFIA BROKE the surface, gasped, and dropped her head back under the water. She'd lost track of how many laps she'd done. The truth was that she had barely been counting in the first place. The past two weeks she'd only kept swimming until her muscles burned too much to continue. She had tried texting Marion a few times with no response. She had reached out to her on MEOW with the same result. Her only other options were stopping by the catering office or her apartment, and both of those options seemed horribly stalkerish.

So she threw herself into work and swimming. She didn't think about what could have been. She ignored how often she found herself thinking about Marion. The dreams didn't help. Torrid fantasies where Reggie transformed into Marion during the act, scenarios that sent her to take a cold shower as soon as she woke up. Occasionally she got angry. Marion could reach out just as easily, could realize she made a horrible mistake, could fix everything. Who did she think she was, just deciding they wouldn't go further in their relationship? Of all the arrogant, self-centered...

She reached the end of the lane and paused to check the room. A few senior citizens had arrived and were stretching at the far side of the pool. That meant aqua aerobics would be starting soon, so she swam back to the other side of the lane and pulled herself up and out. Maybe if the woman from the sauna was back, she would take her up on the offer. Could be all she needed was to get laid, move on, forget Marion Vogt once and for all.

When she finished her routine at the gym, Sofia planned on going directly to work. She had a handful of stories to pitch at the morning meeting and wanted a few minutes to figure out which one was the priority. She stopped to pick up something for lunch so she wouldn't have to track something down in the middle of the day.

Before meeting Marion, she would have been content with a sandwich or something that could be stored in her desk for few hours until she took a break. Now she wanted something more. She wanted something gourmet, something that had been made with care. To be perfectly frank, she wanted a meal similar to what Marion had made for her. She had yet to find anything that came close, but she wasn't prepared to declare defeat.

The night before she'd had a fish sandwich that came closer than anything else. It was a flounder sandwich on a sesame bun with a thick coating of tartar sauce. It was juicy, flavored with lemon and relish and just a dash of Tabasco sauce to give it a kick. She'd savored each bite, licking the excess sauce from the side of the bun. When she rolled a bite of fish over her tongue, she remembered the taste of Marion's mouth when they kissed. It was a mixture of lemon and ice cream, a combination that shouldn't have worked but definitely did. When she sucked the juice from her finger, she remembered the tip of Marion's tongue in her mouth.

She'd masturbated that night imagining a scenario where she hadn't notice the time, where it had been a different date. When she came, she felt guilty. She'd run out on the night, so using it as a fantasy felt wrong. But food was safe. She could enjoy a great meal without feeling guilty. She just had to keep her hands from wandering.

Sofia bought a Turkey and Swiss sub which hopefully wouldn't cause any flashbacks and went to work. She had only just gotten settled in when Del came strolling through the newsroom toward her. She kept her head down in the hopes he'd continue on, but he slowed down next to her desk and stuck both hands in his pockets, obviously waiting for her to finish what she was doing before he interrupted.

"Del, I just got here five minutes ago. Give me a few minutes to get situated before you dump anything else on me, okay?"

"I know when you got here. I asked the receptionist to buzz me when you came in." She looked up at him and saw that he looked uncharacteristically thoughtful. "Do you have a minute?"

She wanted to say no, but she was genuinely curious what was on his mind. "Sure, I can spare a little time before the meeting. What's up?"

He gestured with his head and started walking. Sofia had no choice but to stand and follow him. He led her into the break nook, an open area that couldn't possibly provide more privacy than her desk, and began preparing a cup of coffee.

"You watch FNC, right?"

"No, I get all my news from KCTV Channel Six, the Pacific Northwest's news leader for six years running."

He smirked. "Nice. I didn't even see the station owner's mouth move when you said that. Well, anyway, FNC is doing a new hour-long show on regional topics. Fifteen minutes for New York and the east coast, fifteen minutes for the heartland, et cetera. They needed someone to anchor the west coast segment and I got the call."

"That's great, Del. Congratulations."

Del sipped his coffee. "Congratulations to you, too. I told management about the offer this morning and they asked me to recommend my replacement as head anchor. Turns out my first choice was the same as theirs."

It took her a moment to realize he'd actually suggested her for the job. "You're kidding."

"It's yours if you want it. You have the seniority and the chops for it. Every time they do a focus group, your ratings blow mine out of the water."

"Would I have to stop doing Back-Up?"

He scoffed. "You'll be the star of the show. You can do whatever segments you want." He pushed away from the counter. "The official offer is going to be made tomorrow or Wednesday, but we wanted to give you some time to sleep on it. If you say yes, I'll announce I'm leaving on Friday night's show."

"And if I say no?"

"I'll hold off until we have a replacement ready to go."

Sofia nodded. "Okay. Thanks for the heads-up. And congratulations... did I say that already?"

He smiled. "You did. Coffee?"

"No, thanks. I have a cup of the real stuff at my desk."

He left and Sofia made her way back to her desk. Lead anchor. She was going to be the lead anchor of the Channel Six News. She lowered herself into the seat, grabbed her phone, and stared at the display as she tried to think of who she could call with the news. There was a lot to consider, many pros and cons to weigh, but she would go through all of that with Kathryn. At the moment she wanted to shriek joyfully with someone who would celebrate for her and be proud of her. She thought about texting Kathryn, but she would arrive soon enough and hear the news in person. But beyond her...

There was no one. She imagined Reggie's reaction and tried to think of someone, anyone, in her life who would match that joy. Marion would have been thrilled for her, but that bridge was effectively and completely burned and the ashes were scattered to the winds. Weren't they? She started to type out a text. "I know we didn't end things on the best terms..." She deleted the words and put the phone down.

She stood up and trekked through the warren of corridors in the building until she found Del. He was in the control room sitting in front of a bank of currently-blank monitors. "Hey... what are you doing?"

He gestured at the controls in front of him. "Just taking the place in, hoping I remember everything. I worked here a long time and hardly ever came back here."

"Oh. Listen, when you announce you're leaving, is the station going to throw a big party for you? A farewell and a celebration of your years working here?"

"They'd damn well better," he said, smiling.

Sofia nodded. "Right. When the time comes, I know who they can hire for catering. Beacon Craft and Catering Service."

He tilted his head to the side. "Aren't they the place you took down a few months ago? You trying to give me food poisoning, Sofe?"

"They were cleared for that," Sofia said. "It wasn't their fault. And I've had their food since then. It's phenomenal. Just be sure they hire them, okay?"

"Okay. My going-away party will double as a congratulatory event for you, so if this is a trick, it'll backfire."

"Trust me," Sofia said, "you'll love it."

He was making a note on his phone as she left. She didn't know if that counted as stalker behavior. Maybe it was right on the line, maybe it was over the line, but she didn't care. In a few weeks she and Marion would be in the same place at the same time without making it confrontational. She had that much time to figure out how she was going to take advantage of that scenario.

In the weeks after her aborted fling with Sofia, Marion estimated she worked more events than she ever had as a waitress. She assigned herself to anything that would be light on manpower, and there were more events for her crews to be spread out across. Storybook Farm apparently liked them well enough to leave them on the list of approved vendors. Beacon had been the caterers for three weddings with four more booked. She was thinking about putting out an ad for more waiters just to keep up with the demand.

She smiled when the topic came up, still remembering her panic when Sofia's report first ran. At one point she almost picked up the phone to brag to Sofia, a friendly ribbing, but she stopped herself before she dialed. Courtney appeared in the doorway of her office as she was staring at the phone.

"Everything okay?"

Marion nodded. "Yeah. What's up?"

"I need your input." Marion gestured at the seat across from her and Courtney came in. "We got a request to do a sit-down dinner for sixty guests two weeks from Friday."

"Okay."

"For Channel Six."

Marion blinked. "What's the occasion?"

"One of their anchors is leaving for cable news. Not Sofia."

Marion tried to act nonchalant. "What? I mean, I don't care."

Courtney said, "Sure you don't. It's her co-anchor, Del Stockton. But Sofia is probably going to be there, too. I just wanted to be sure it was okay with you if we booked it."

"Why wouldn't it be?"

Courtney stared at her.

"It's a job. It's just another event."

"Marion, come on."

Marion sighed and adjusted things on her desk to look busy. "What? We had a few dates, we butted heads a few times, and it's done."

Courtney said, "Okay. It's done. Say, how have things been on MEOW? Met anyone lately?"

"I haven't looked at it."

"Oh, but you've been going out, right?"

Marion said, "When exactly would I have had time to go out?

We've been busy as hell the past few weeks. I only go home to sleep and change clothes."

"So you haven't gone out with anybody since Sofia. But you're totally over her."

"There's nothing to get over," Marion said. "Accept the job if we're free on that night. Hell, I'll even work the damn thing to prove to you that it's not a big deal."

Courtney said, "I'm going to call your bluff."

"Good. Call it. I don't care."

"Okay." Courtney stood and left the office.

Marion immediately realized it was a dumb idea. She was obviously hung up on Sofia. She even messaged Penny and regretfully informed her that she wasn't currently feeling up to even a casual get-together anytime soon. It sucked that she felt like she was recovering from a relationship when she didn't even have the benefit of getting laid, but that was exactly her situation. It didn't help that Sofia seemed to be on the news every time Marion turned on the TV. Either a broadcast or a commercial, a bumper at the end of a TV show she was watching... And then there were the advertisements on bus stop benches and the trolley. There didn't seem to be any escape from her.

She decided working the Channel Six event would be the best way to finally put Sofia behind her. She'd built up a false Sofia in her mind and seeing her again in person would help dispel that image. Like when a song was stuck in her head, all she had to do was listen to the song in full and it would vanish. The odds were good that one of them would say the wrong thing and reignite the irritation and dislike that defined their earlier interactions. It would be a lot easier to hate Sofia than... to feel whatever it was she was feeling.

When she left work, she went to the bar. She told herself she was going to pick up the first woman who appealed to her, take her home, and ravish her. It was supposed to be part of healing, of getting the "Sofia song" out of her head. But no one stuck out to her, not even the gorgeous blonde who bought her a beer. There was a brunette who looked like Sofia, who might have acted as a glorious substitute, but after five minutes of conversation she said those dreaded words: "So, my boyfriend is over there. He would think it was really hot if..."

In the end, Marion went home alone. She masturbated in the shower and pampered herself with the good soaps. When she got out of the shower, she wrapped herself in the fluffiest robe she owned and let her hair dry naturally. She sat on the foot of her bed to put lotion on her hands and the last prime-time show ended with a segue to the news. Her hands were slick with the lotion so she couldn't grab the remote, and she sneered at the screen as Sofia and Del Stockton appeared.

"Welcome to Channel Six News, I'm Del Stockton."

"And I'm Sofia Kennedy. We begin tonight with breaking news..."

Marion had her hands in her lap. As she watched, she turned one hand over and smoothed her fingers over the inside of her thigh. She ignored what Sofia was saying and focused on her eyes. Less than a month ago, this woman had been in her apartment. Touching her. Kissing her through her clothes. Marion very vividly remembered the touch of Sofia's hands, the way her mouth had felt on her throat. Those lips on TV right now had parted and that tongue had touched Marion's mouth.

She had her hand completely between her legs now, leaning back slightly, not quite touching herself but unable to deny her intent if anyone caught her. God, she'd been ready. She closed her eyes and tried to imagine how it would have gone. The fingers of her other hand, stretched out behind her for support, curled in the duvet. She was still tingling from the orgasm she'd given herself in the shower so it didn't take much effort for her to climax again.

When she finished she climaxed, red-cheeked and crossing her legs over her hand. She cleared her throat and looked at the TV almost bashfully as if Sofia could see what she had done.

The image shifted to a full shot of Sofia, her face initially turned down to look at the desk. She raised her eyes first, looking through her lashes and smiling slightly into the lens. Marion's breath caught and she tightened her thighs around her hand. That smile, that sparkle in her eyes... there was no way she could actually *know* what had just happened. No. No, she was reacting to something in the story. She teased the next story and looked down again as the image faded out. Marion let out a breath she didn't realize she'd been holding.

She couldn't break this woman's spell fast enough.

CHAPTER TWENTY-ONE

MARION HAD accepted years ago how odd her job was. She put on a uniform and went out to deliver plate upon plate of the finest food to people dressed in tuxedos and gowns. Her workplace changed on a daily basis but she was almost always working somewhere lavish and fairy-tale gorgeous. She saw people on the greatest days of their lives when they put the maximum effort into every part of their appearance. It would be easy to imagine that the whole world was like that, glitzy and glamorous while she toiled away in the kitchen, but she knew the truth and could appreciate her place in their sparkling world.

She rode in the front of the lead van, the covered dishes clanking on the shelves behind her as Courtney drove them around to the back entrance. They'd worked the venue before, a renovated factory on the western shore of Lake Union. The private event area was in the mezzanine and had a sweeping panoramic view of the lake. Courtney parked and worked with Tyrone to get the vans unloaded into the kitchen. Marion went to find the event coordinator and let him know they'd arrived.

The Channel Six team had gone all out for Del Stockton, honoring the eighteen years he'd been a staple of Seattle's news scene. The room was full of tables decorated in silver and red, the channel's unofficial colors, and the podium on the main stage was flanked by large headshots of the man himself. Marion passed by the tables on the stage and saw one place was marked for Sofia Kennedy, the seat just to the right of the podium, and she felt oddly proud of Sofia.

I can feel proud for her, she told herself. *Just because whatever we planned to do fizzled out doesn't mean I hate her.*

She found the event coordinator and then went to help her crew prepare. She was almost to the kitchen when she crossed paths with the woman herself. Sofia Kennedy in full regalia, dressed to the nines in a black gown with silver accents on the bodice. Marion half-expected to see a group of servants carrying her train. Sofia was half-turned away to speak with someone behind her and there was a moment when Marion could have escaped notice. A door to her left led into a meeting room where she could hide until Sofia passed. But she was frozen to the spot by the beauty of the other woman and was still standing there when Sofia turned and spotted her.

"Miss Vogt."

She felt a shudder at that and hoped it didn't show on her face. "Miss Kennedy."

"I'm glad you're here." Sofia's eyes tracked the people she'd come in with until they were gone. She stepped closer to Marion and lowered her voice. "I wanted to talk to you."

"I think it would be better if we just avoided each other, don't you?"

"No." Sofia sighed and looked at the ground. "There's going to be a big speech by Del toward the end of the night. He's going to ask me to say a few words. Will you please be there for that? I want you to hear what I have to say."

Marion nodded. "Sure."

"Okay. We can talk after if you want."

"Okay," Marion said, although she envisioned herself making the quickest escape possible once her catering duties were complete.

Sofia touched Marion's arm. "It's great to see you again. I've missed you."

"I've missed you, too," Marion admitted. "But nothing's changed, has it?"

"We'll talk after the party," Sofia said.

"Sure."

Sofia walked away and Marion turned to watch her go. That ass... god. She pushed thoughts of Sofia's anatomy out of her mind and went to work.

Sit-down dinners were relatively easy. No circulating with appetizers, no trays of drinks to balance as they bobbed and weaved through a crowd of attendees. They just had to keep an eye out for anyone who needed their drinks freshened or their plates cleared. Marion found a position to the right of the stage where she could keep an eye on everything. Her head moved on a swivel, her eyes skimming over everyone like a Secret Service agent looking for a threat.

The party included a long montage of Del's various highlights through his two decades of service. His first major story was covering the Battle of Seattle, and his position as a Seattle institution was sealed a few years later during the Mardi Gras riots. The audience laughed at the montage showing his attempt to walk across Seattle with a cup of Starbucks coffee that could never be empty for more than one city block. He'd succeeded, but only barely. The clips replayed his heartfelt pleas for the city to keep the Supersonics, a bid that eventually failed, and the night he honored the one hundred and twentieth anniversary of the Great Seattle Fire by doing a broadcast as an 1889 newsman reporting the events live.

His fellow anchors took the podium to simultaneously honor and roast Del. Sofia was the last to take the podium, and Marion took her attention off the diners to watch her.

"I learned everything I know about journalism and television news from this man. Which means I really wasted all that money going to school." Marion chuckled and brushed her hand over her mouth to hide it. "I'm not good at the all-in-fun ribbing everyone else has been doing tonight. I've been told I tend to get too mean." She rolled her eyes and shrugged. The audience laughed. "So to spare him tonight, I'm not even going to try. I'm just going to sincerely say that Del has helped me get through some very hard broadcasts, and it will be very hard walking out on that set and not seeing him sitting there to watch my back. To you, Del."

"Hear, hear," Evan said.

The audience toasted. Del stood and hugged Sofia, then held up a hand to cut off the applause. "Sofia, don't sit down just yet. You're not done talking. The bigwigs at the studio were kind enough to ask my opinion about who should fill my seat. It's a big responsibility and I knew that only the best journalist deserved a chance at it. Fortunately, she agreed to take the job. Ladies and gentlemen, please continue applauding for the new face of Channel

Six News, Miss Sofia Kennedy."

The applause resumed. Sofia looked uncharacteristically shy under the onslaught of attention. She nudged Del with her shoulder and he smiled at her as he joined the applause.

"And now she's going to say a few words, whether she wants to or not."

The audience laughed as Del sat down. "This isn't fair. No one else had to give two speeches." More laughter. "First, I want to thank everyone for this tremendous honor. Del, you made that seat important and I'm going to do my best to honor the legacy you established. Secondly, to the people of Seattle. You've always counted on me to tell you the truth. You trusted me even when I haven't been entirely truthful with you." She rested her hands on the podium and braced herself. "So even knowing that this might change how people see me, there's something I have to say..."

"Oh, no," Marion whispered. She was going to come out. Marion was moving as Sofia raised her head and opened her mouth to begin speaking again. She stepped onto the stage and rushed forward. "False alarm! It's a false alarm. Sorry."

Sofia turned to her, as did every head in the room. The anchors onstage twisted to look at the unexpected interruption as Marion stopped next to Sofia, who was frowning at her.

Marion's smile was almost a grimace, her eyes wide and unblinking as she looked at the event she had just brought to a screeching halt. Catering 101, never interrupt the event.

"False alarm," she said again. "I-I was... I'm the, uh, the caterer, uh, Marion Vogt. I asked So— Miss Kennedy if she would make an announcement that we were running low on chardonnay. But we just found a, uh, a full crate of it in one of the vans, so there's plenty to go around for everyone. I feel bad for putting her on the spot like that, but I didn't realize how dramatic she would make it."

Sofia stared at Marion for just a moment too long, completely thrown off her script and trying to hide it. She smiled nervously and gestured at the crowd. "Well, I know how much these folks like their liquor."

The audience laughed.

Marion didn't know how to get off-stage gracefully, so she simply lifted her hand in an awkward wave and fled. She heard Sofia's voice through the PA system as she escaped.

"Well, bullet dodged, I suppose. I... what I was... uh..."

Marion stopped in the shadows next to the stage and watched.

Sofia looked as if she might carry on with what she was going to say, but then shook her head.

"Well, I guess what I was saying was that I-I'm thankful for this opportunity. If I can do half the job Del has done, I can consider myself a success."

The audience applauded. Sofia moved to take her seat and noticed Marion watching her. Marion gestured with her head and Sofia gave the slightest of nods to show she understood. Marion walked away, still shaking from what had almost happened, and went through a side door that led out onto a small covered walkway. She hugged herself against the breeze coming off the lake and looked at the boats out on the water, swaying on the gentle crest of each wave. She didn't have to wait long until the door opened and Sofia joined her outside.

"What the hell was that?" Sofia whispered.

"You're asking me? What were you about to do?"

Sofia said, "I was going to show you how much I care about you. I spent my entire relationship hiding Reggie, ignoring how special she was to me. I spent five years with her and no one in that room knows her name."

"You think that's what I wanted?" Marion asked. It was a struggle to keep her voice down, emotions boiling under the surface. "I'm not trying to win some contest with Reggie. I'm not trying to erase how special she was to you. She'll always be an important part of your life. I just wanted you to acknowledge that you were holding on to the past so tightly that you weren't letting yourself live in the present. Never let go of Reggie. Just don't let her blind you to what you might be missing here and now."

Sofia said, "That's what I was trying to prove in there."

"I appreciate the gesture, Sofia, I do, but that is not what I want. You live in the public eye. It makes sense that you'd want something that is private, that's just for you. Reggie was precious. She belonged to just you, not everyone in there or anyone who happened to see you on the news." She took Sofia's hand. "Don't take such a drastic step to prove a point to me, or for any reason other than being ready. If you truly want to live openly and freely, then fine. Go back in there and wave your rainbow flag all over the place. But I don't think that's what you actually want."

"There's only one thing I want," Sofia said, "and she's standing right in front of me. I'm willing to do whatever it takes to make her understand that."

Marion closed her eyes. "Sofia... I can't..."

"No, listen, you were right. I let Reggie become a minefield for you. That wasn't fair to you or to her memory. I was using her as an excuse to stay stuck in the past. So from here on out, I'm celebrating differently. I'm not going to hide on days that were special to us. I'm going to use them as touchstones to do something to move on. It's what Reggie would have wanted. And she really would have wanted me to stay at your apartment the other night."

Marion opened her eyes and looked at Sofia. "Yeah?"

"Yeah. I realized that above all else, she would want me to be happy. Since she can't be here for me, she would want me to be with someone like you."

"Don't run away again. Talk to me. If you start to panic, if you think something is going wrong, sit your ass down and talk to me about it. Give me a chance to work through it with you."

Sofia nodded. "Yes."

"If you run again, I'm letting you go."

"I understand. I'm not going anywhere."

Marion cupped Sofia's cheek. "I wish I could kiss you right now."

"I wish that, too." She put her hand on Marion's hip and they moved closer to each other. Marion could hear traffic on the street and was all too aware of the possibility someone could walk down the wrong corridor and see them through the window. She brushed her thumb over Sofia's cheek and then dropped her hand.

"I should probably let you get back to the party..."

"My part of it is over. There's mingling, maybe some dancing. I just sit there and wait for everyone to start going home. But you need to get back to work."

Marion said, "Courtney and Tyrone are both here. They can cover anything that comes up."

They stared at each other.

Sofia said, "I could leave early. No one would care."

"Could I get a ride?"

"Absolutely."

They went back inside. Marion hurried to the kitchen and found Courtney was already in full command of the team. She put a hand on her elbow and leaned in close.

"Hey... can you and Ty handle things here for the rest of the event?"

"Sure. Are you okay?"

"I'm fine."

Courtney lowered her voice further. "A few of the waiters saw what happened. We're not even close to running out of chardonnay. What really happened out there?"

"Nothing."

"And now you're running off, even though you're fine."

Marion nodded. "Uh-huh."

Courtney narrowed her eyes. "If I was a mean person, I would refuse to take over until you told me the whole story."

"Lucky for me." Marion leaned in and kissed Courtney's cheek. "Thank you."

"Just promise me it's for a good reason."

Marion hesitated. "I think so. I think it's a really, really good reason. I have hope."

"Then get out of here. We'll keep the ship sailing."

"Thank you, Courtney."

Courtney saluted. Marion turned and fled the kitchen, moving through a hallway that ran alongside the main room. When she got to the main entrance she saw Sofia was waiting for her. Now that she didn't have to fight her reactions, she could admit how utterly gorgeous she looked. The light coming through the glass surrounded her in a pale yellow aura that reflected off the darkness of her hair and gown, sparkling off the silver accents to draw the eye to her chest. Not that Marion needed the prompting.

Sofia turned at the sound of Marion's approach and smiled nervously. "I told them I wasn't feeling well. I hope it doesn't reflect poorly on your catering."

Marion took Sofia's hand, guiding her out into the parking lot. "The last time you badmouthed me, business started booming. So by all means."

Sofia smirked and let herself be dragged outside. "I'm parked over here."

With the way traffic usually was at this time of day, it would take close to twenty minutes for them to get back to Marion's apartment. She hoped they would be able to contain themselves until then, or else Channel Six's traffic segment would get very graphic.

CHAPTER TWENTY-TWO

MARION LET them into her apartment and shut the door. Sofia hesitated, unsure if they were going to pick up where they left off the last time, but Marion set her mind at ease by kissing her. They easily fell into an embrace. Sofia let Marion turn her and press her against the wall, sliding her hand down the middle of Marion's back to where her uniform shirt was tucked into her slacks. Marion's hands roamed Sofia's back in search of a zipper or hooks that could release the material. Sofia was lost in the kiss, trying to remember if their kiss the other night, the night she ruined, had been half as good as this one. Then suddenly it was over, Marion was stepping back, her hands dropping away.

Sofia opened her eyes. "If this was all just a tease, I'm going to cry."

Marion smiled in the dark. "No. Sorry. Just a second." She crossed the room and closed the blinds that looked out onto the neighboring building. On her way back she turned on the light using a dimmer switch that kept the room mostly in shadow. She walked back to Sofia and placed her palms flat on her chest. She looked into Sofia's eyes and slid her hands up, over her neck to the back of her head, pulling her closer ever so slowly.

"I think it's been a long time since you had a safe place. I think you've been looking since Reggie died. I want this to be your safe place, Sofia."

Their lips were touching by the last word, and Sofia moaned as she turned the sentiment into a kiss. Marion's hands were in her hair, untangling the twists and braids the station's stylist had spent an hour putting into place. She curled her fingers, untucked Marion's shirt, and reached underneath to stroke the warm skin of her lower back. Marion gave up working on the hooks of Sofia's dress and moved her hands lower, cupping her ass and squeezing gently.

Marion kissed away from Sofia's mouth, moving along her cheek to find her ear. Sofia took the opportunity to kiss and nuzzle Marion's throat while Marion nipped at her earlobe.

"Pull up your dress," Marion whispered.

She felt Sofia shiver, and then her hands disappeared from Marion's backside. Sofia swayed slightly from side-to-side as she inched her dress up her thighs and over her hips, her breath rough against Marion's neck as she obeyed her directive. Marion reached down and brushed her palms over the newly-exposed skin, pushing up the loose hem of the slip and feeling the top of Sofia's stockings. Sofia gasped and pressed her lips to Marion's neck.

"I want to know what you taste like."

Sofia's voice shook when she said, "Then find out..."

Marion pulled back and unfastened her belt, then unbuttoned her pants. The material went loose around her waist as she kissed her way down Sofia's chest and crouched in front of her. Sofia whispered for her to wait and stepped out of her heels. She lost the advantage of height and rested her hands on Marion's shoulders. Marion lifted the dress and slip out of the way and kissed the material of Sofia's underwear. She stroked the inside of Sofia's thigh with one hand, then turned her wrist and cupped Sofia with her palm.

Marion's other hand moved to her own lap, pushing into her trousers to touch herself as she moved the underwear out of her way and wet her lips. She could smell Sofia as her lips made contact, her tongue pushing out to drag across Sofia's folds. She teased herself with her middle finger and closed her eyes. Sofia moved her hands into Marion's hair and leaned heavily against the wall. She rolled her hips forward, knees bent, thighs shaking as Marion alternated between using the tip and flat of her tongue to massage the sensitive flesh.

"Please don't stop," Sofia whispered. Then she added, "Miss

Vogt."

Marion groaned and redoubled her efforts. Sofia grunted in response, undoing Marion's braids with trembling hands. Her hair fell in tangles and curls until there was enough of it for Sofia to run through her fingers.

"Are you touching yourself, Miss Vogt?"

"Mm..."

"Good..."

Marion looked up, watching Sofia's face. The dim lighting cast angular shadows across her face, her eyebrows arched in twisted lines. Her lips were parted and trembled with each breath. Marion pulled back and wet her fingers in her mouth. She cupped Sofia's sex again and looked up at her as she slipped her middle finger inside.

"You're going to come for me, Sofia."

"Yes..."

Marion leaned in again and found Sofia's clit. She closed her mouth around it as she added a second finger, and Sofia's hands curled in Marion's hair. She gasped without words, one leg coming up as if she wanted to wrap it around Marion's head. She rocked her hips forward and then back against the wall, making inarticulate sounds of pleasure as she flattened her hand to stroke Marion's hair.

"God... my god... wow..."

Marion took her hand from her pants and kissed her way back up Sofia's body. Sofia cupped Marion's face and kissed her hard even as her body seemed to go limp, supported only by the wall and Marion's hand on her waist. Sofia gently sucked on Marion's tongue before the kiss ended.

"You eat as well as you cook."

Marion laughed. "Thank you. How about you? Does that mouth only work on television?"

"I'll show you. Did you come?"

"No."

Sofia took her hand. "Let's take care of that. Take me to the bedroom."

Marion led Sofia through the apartment, her pants awkwardly sagging as they went into the bedroom. She left the light off and sat on the bed. Sofia climbed onto her lap, pushing her back onto the mattress. She met Marion's stare as she dropped her hand to the knot in her tie, tugging it loose before she started working on the buttons.

"I want you naked, Miss Vogt."

Marion ran her hands up Sofia's thighs, then around to her back. "If I ever figure out these goddamn hooks..."

Sofia smiled and pushed open Marion's shirt. When she bent down to kiss her chest, Marion lifted her head to see what her hands were doing. She managed to get the dress undone by some miracle, her brain rebelling at mechanical thoughts while Sofia's tongue was moving along the edge of her bra. Sofia felt the dress go slack around her and hunched her shoulders so Marion could pull it away as she sat up. She unhooked her own bra and let it fall, settling her weight on Marion's stomach.

"I masturbated when I watched you on the news," Marion said.

"Was it good?"

"Mm-hmm." She bit her bottom lip and pulled her arms out of her shirt, leaving it underneath her as she undid her bra.

Sofia finished taking off Marion's tie. "Good. I practically came every time I had a good meal. Imagining your fingers in the meat... measuring out the spices. I could almost taste you."

Marion said, "Take off my pants, Sofia."

"Yes, Miss Vogt." She moved so she could get the pants off, yanking off her shoes and socks in the same movement. She took off her dress as well, leaving her in stockings.

"Leave those on."

"Yeah?" Sofia said.

"Oh, yeah."

Sofia put her hand on Marion's foot and eased her legs apart so she could lie between them. Marion pulled Sofia to her and they kissed as she lifted her feet. She hooked them at the ankles behind Sofia's back and pushed her down until she felt Sofia pressing against her. Sofia placed her hands on the mattress and began to thrust, her hip sliding against Marion's sex. Marion closed her eyes and rested her hands on Sofia's shoulders, grunting quietly in her throat as she let Sofia set the rhythm. Sofia began kissing her face. A peck on the cheek, another on either closed eye, just below her hair. Marion kept her hands moving, exploring the lines and curves of Sofia's body before moving down to her ass.

"This..." Sofia whispered, then put her head down on Marion's shoulder.

"What?" Marion whispered. Sofia's hair was covering her face.

"I don't know what I was going to say." Sofia was breathless.

Instead of speaking, she turned her head and kissed Marion's neck. Her hand moved between their bodies and she brushed her hands through Marion's pubic hair. When she slid lower, Marion gasped and arched her back. Her toes curled and her arms and legs tightened around Sofia.

"More..."

Sofia moved faster and unfolded a second finger. Marion bared her teeth and twisted her head. She sat up in search of Sofia's mouth. Sofia found her halfway and kissed her as she came, stifling her moans as she rolled her hip so it rubbed magnificently against her now-extremely sensitive parts, making her gasp and groan through a series of aftershocks. She closed her teeth on Sofia's bottom lip and pulled gently before soothing the reddened skin with her tongue. Sofia relaxed and settled on top of Marion, who cupped the back of her head and stroked her back. The room was silent except for the sound of them catching their breath.

"Am I too heavy?" Sofia whispered.

"No. I like it."

"I want to go to sleep."

Marion turned her head and kissed Sofia's hair. "Then sleep. I'll be here."

"Marion..."

Her voice trailed off even before she finished saying her name, so whatever she planned to say afterward was lost. Marion didn't care. She closed her eyes and listened to the sound of Sofia breathing.

It was dark when Sofia woke up. She looked at the window, vaguely differentiated from the other darkness by the pale yellow glow of a streetlight. She was alone in bed but she could hear movement in the other room. The room smelled of sweat and sex, with the added element of Marion's personal scent underneath it. There was also another odor coming from the other room, evidence that Marion was cooking something. She stretched under the blanket she assumed Marion had covered her with, curling her toes and pressing her hands against the headboard.

She tried to compare how she felt to the various one-night stands since Reggie, but she couldn't. There was something ineffably different about the situations. In the past she went home with women to get sex. She was only interested in getting off and getting out. There was the biological need to be with another person, and the person's identity was just a matter of aesthetics. She liked to be with attractive people, sure, but beyond that they were interchangeable.

Marion flipped everything around. With Marion, sex was the tool. Sex was what she used to connect herself to this other woman, this woman who had ignited such feelings of rage and fury inside of her. Moreover, she didn't want to flee. Leaving the apartment was the furthest thing on her mind, even if they didn't have sex again. She just wanted to share the same space. That was huge.

Finally, she decided to go investigate the source of the cooking smells. She didn't want to put her dress back on, and fortunately Marion's uniform blouse was crumpled on the floor next to the bed. Sofia slipped it on and, despite the difference in their sizes, managed to button enough of it for modesty. She found her panties and put them on, took off her stockings, and ventured barefoot out into the main room.

Marion was at the stove in a T-shirt that was just short enough to reveal she wasn't wearing anything else. Her hair was pulled back but still managed to look sloppy. Music was playing so softly that Sofia hadn't heard it from the other room. Marion looked up from what she was cooking and smiled.

"Hey."

"Hey yourself," Sofia said.

Marion gestured at the stove. "I made enough for two. I just hadn't eaten anything all night."

"Caterers don't get to graze the entrees?"

"Well, from time to time," Marion said with a smile. She stirred the food. "How was your nap?"

Sofia sat on one of the stools at the counter. "It was fine, but I think I preferred everything that happened pre-nap."

Marion grinned. "I enjoyed that, too."

"What are you cooking? It smells delicious."

"I didn't have much on-hand. I just threw together some things from the pantry. Some enchiladas with basil and oregano."

"That's something you just threw together from the pantry?"

Marion shrugged as she prepared a plate. "The hazards of dating a chef." She hesitated as she put a plate in front of Sofia. "Not that we're... I mean, after what happened, you can see why I might assume, but I don't expect..."

"Marion," Sofia said gently. She was looking at the plate to avoid meeting Marion's gaze. "If you'll have me, I would be lucky to be with you."

"Of course I'll have you." She came around the counter and touched Sofia's chin. "Just remember what we talked about."

"Talk. Don't run."

Marion nodded and leaned in. They kissed softly, and Sofia could taste spices from an enchilada on Marion's lips.

"Mm. That makes me hungry."

Marion smiled and gestured at the plate. "Then dig in. And afterward, I have some clothes you can borrow if you want to go home."

"And if I want to stay here?"

"Then I've planned a lot of fun things to do with your naked body."

Sofia grinned wickedly and moved her plate closer. She wanted to eat quickly so they could get back to bed as quickly as possible. She wanted to know what Marion's plans were.

CHAPTER TWENTY-THREE

SOFIA SPENT the night and, in the morning, borrowed a T-shirt and jeans to wear home. She gathered her clothes from the night before and tried not to imagine being spotted on the street. Sofia Kennedy, newly-promoted anchor of the Channel Six News, doing the walk of shame. How much detective work would it take to find out where she'd come from or who she'd left the party with? In the end, she decided she didn't care. She would stay in the closet for the time being and not worry about being found out.

Over breakfast, Sofia warned Marion that she might be hard to reach for the next few days. "I don't want you to freak out and think I'm running away. I just foresee a ton of meetings and brainstorming sessions at the station, not to mention those cutesy bits we'll probably record. Commercials about my new position..." Her shoulders slumped. "God, I'm exhausted just thinking about it."

"I understand," Marion said. "When I took over Beacon, it felt like two whole months just vanished into the ether. I'll be here when you take a breath. Besides, we have some things to work out ourselves. Some very important matters to discuss."

Sofia said, "For instance?"

"Which side of the bed do you prefer? I like the window side."

Sofia looked past Marion into the bedroom to remind herself

which side had the window. She nodded. "I can go along with that. Are you big spoon or little spoon?"

"I like being the little spoon," Marion said, with just a hint of bashfulness. "But I can hold you I you need me to."

It was a simple offer, but Sofia felt warmth spreading through her chest. "That's good to know." She stirred her cereal, the least culinary meal Marion had ever given her. "And I guess we should talk about the dynamics of dating someone in my situation. We can't exactly go out to dinner and you won't be hanging off my arm at events like last night's."

"That's fine. I'll probably be working most events like last night's."

Sofia said, "Well, if I have any say in it, you will. Are you going to be okay with that?"

Marion said, "I've dated women in the closet before. I can figure things out."

"Okay. I should probably..."

"Yeah..." Marion slid off her stool and walked Sofia to the door. "Should we... I mean, do we kiss goodbye, or...?"

"Of course." Sofia brushed her hand down Marion's arm as they kissed. "I'll call or text you sometime."

Marion nodded. "Okay."

Sofia took her dress from the night before and left before she could be tempted to stay. She waited until she was safely in her car before she checked her messages. One from Del, a few from various friends and colleagues at the station congratulating her, dozens from people she didn't recognize. As she scrolled through the notifications she realized that her phone must have been buzzing almost constantly while she and Marion were advancing their relationship. She was grateful that she'd turned it to silent before the ceremony.

The only messages she felt like returning were Kathryn's. The earliest ones were the expected notes of congratulations and queries about grabbing some 'real food' after the party. Then there were a handful of 'where did you disappear to?' questions and requests for a sign of life. The last one made her feel guilty: "I'm worried. Not 'call the police' worried, but 'I'll be pissed when it turns out you're fine' worried. Call me. Text me. Let me know you're okay. Love you."

She dialed Kathryn and looked out the window as the ringtone buzzed in her ear. Kathryn answered on the second tone.

"It's about goddamn time, Sofia."

"I was getting laid."

The anger vanished from Kathryn's voice. "What? Really? Okay. Hold on. Let me switch gears. You went home with someone? Who's the lucky lady?"

"The caterer."

"The..." Kathryn laughed. "Of course. How did it go?"

Sofia started to answer, giving in to the typical gossip of the morning after, but the words got caught in her throat. She closed her eyes and bowed her head as she tried to compose her thoughts. Her fingers tightened on the phone as she rested her other arm on the steering wheel so she could lean forward and rest her head on it.

"It went right. It went... really, really right."

"I'm glad to hear that, Sofe," Kathryn said softly. "I really am. You deserve it. How are you feeling with the whole... guilt situation? Any lingering anxiety?"

Sofia said, "No. I think the only thing I regret is that I didn't do it sooner."

"Well, you couldn't do it sooner. You didn't know the caterer, whose name I can't remember at the moment, and you needed to chip through that armor you'd put up after you lost Reggie. You know why it hurt so bad? Because you were just an exposed nerve getting hit by the air. You needed time to get used to living without keeping the walls up all the time."

"Yeah." Sofia wiped a hand over her cheeks. "I want to talk to you about all of this, but face to face. And at length, when we're both fully awake."

"Didn't get a lot of sleep last night, huh?"

Sofia rolled her eyes. "You're a child."

Kathryn mimicked squeaking bedsprings. "Oh, caterer... oh, caterer!"

Sofia laughed. "See if I ever tell you my secrets again. Kathryn... thank you. I'm not ready to be completely out yet, but having a friend like you I can confide in is a godsend."

"I'm honored you trust me enough. I'll call you later."

"Okay. Oh... hey..."

"Yeah?"

Sofia looked up at the building and smiled. "Marion. Her name is Marion Vogt."

A man was sitting on a milk crate that had been placed over a musical note painted on the ground. He was strumming a guitar while an iPod hooked to his vest pocket played the backing instruments. Marion stopped and listened to him for a bit, admiring the technological upgrade to the one-man-band before she placed a few dollars into his open case. He nodded his thanks to her and she smiled as she moved on. She admired him for being out in such punishing weather. Winter had decided to slam Seattle once more, and she was bundled in a parka and knit cap, a scarf bundled around her shoulders so thick that it seemed as if she didn't have a neck.

Marion found Sofia by the fish market, well away from where she might get hit by any low-flying fish. She was picking out what she wanted Marion to cook her for dinner. It had been four weeks and three days since their first night together and, true to her warning, Sofia was almost invisible for all of it. Her schedule was one reason their one-month anniversary dinner had been delayed. Marion hadn't exactly been sitting around her apartment staring at the walls. Beacon continued to thrive, and now the Seattle elite who attended the Channel Six event were now calling to hire them for other events.

The few nights they had managed to spend together had been phenomenal. They were still learning and figuring each other out, but the sex was definitely in Marion's top ten. Maybe top five. There was just something special when she was with Sofia. It was something she hadn't felt with anyone else she'd ever slept with. She would call it magic, but that sounded so hokey and cliché that she could barely stand the thought.

But then she spotted Sofia next to the vegetables and had to stop walking so she wouldn't trip over her own feet. Sofia was speaking to the merchant, pointing at something as she asked a question. She was also bundled up in a bright red jacket and a black scarf, her hands kept warm by black leather gloves. She picked up an apple, red and shining despite the season, and seemed to be weighing it in her hand as she scanned the rest of the shop's wares.

She had been in profile but she turned fully toward Marion, revealing her face full-on, and Marion saw the full spectrum of her new lover: the rage of their earliest encounters, the resignation and frustration of their repeated meetings, the raw lust and pleasure she displayed when she was in Marion's bed. Everything and every facet was gorgeous to her now, and even the memory of being hit by a box of tissues made her smile.

She ducked her chin under the barrier of her scarf as she approached. Before she could make Sofia aware of her return, however, a tall black woman in a yellow jacket reached out and touched Sofia's arm. "Sofia?" she asked as Marion took a step back so she wouldn't get caught in an awkward three-way conversation. "Sofia Kennedy?"

Sofia turned and her face brightened. "Renee! When did you get back to Seattle?"

They hugged. "Just three days ago. Long enough to see your gorgeous face all over the news. Congratulations, you. Lead anchor. Quite a coup!"

"Thank you," Sofia said, finally noticing Marion lurking. "Oh! Renee, this is my friend, Marion. Marion, this is Renee. We went to college together."

Marion smiled and offered her hand. "Hi."

"Hello!" Renee still seemed breathless and wide-eyed. "I can't believe I'm just running into you like this. I kept trying to think of how I could get in touch with you. We have to have dinner sometime. When are you free?"

Sofia said, "I'm busy tonight. And tomorrow and..."

"Yeah, yeah, stop bragging. I'm here until Friday. Hopefully we can find a time that works for both of us." They exchanged phone numbers and email addresses before she hugged Sofia again. "God, it's great to see you again. Marion, it was nice meeting you, as brief as it was."

"You too," Marion said.

Sofia and her friend said goodbye and the yellow coat faded back into the crowd. Sofia turned, stared at Marion for ten full seconds, and then faced the grocery shelves.

"I'm not sure what the best side dish would be with what we already have. Expert opinion?"

"Let's see," Marion said.

They ended up with a bag of produce that Marion promised she could turn into a delicious side dish for that evening. Sofia had grown quiet after their encounter with Renee. Marion tried to draw her out but, after a few attempts, decided to let her brood. Their plan had been to shop early, spend the middle of the day holed up in Marion's apartment, and then dinner. It was her hope that Sofia would get over whatever was bothering her in time to salvage their day.

She took the groceries into the kitchen and began unloading

them. Sofia lingered by the door and finally stormed over.

"It doesn't make you angry at all?"

"What doesn't?"

"'My friend, Marion'. I introduced you as my friend."

Marion said, "I assume she didn't know you were gay. Besides, we were in a public space. I didn't even notice it."

"Well, you should have."

Marion pulled an onion from the bag and stared at it. "Wait... are you mad because I'm not mad?"

"I'm mad because you don't care."

"It's not that I don't care. I respect that you have to keep this private and I don't mind it. I know how you really feel."

Sofia said, "It sucks."

"It does suck. I'll agree with you on that. I wish we could just be honest and secure in the knowledge people will respect your privacy. If anything, I'm mad at the people who would demand to know the intimate details of your life just because you happen to be on television. But I'm not angry at you. I'm not holding that against you."

Sofia worried her bottom lip with her teeth. "Good. Because you're more than my friend."

"I know," Marion said softly.

"I love you." Marion stopped again, this time staring at a few stalks of celery. "Don't say it back immediately. I never understood why so many people treat it like a call-and-answer sort of thing. I've only said it to a few people in my life. No one since Regina. I just wanted you to know. For those moments when I don't act like it, or if you feel like I'm dismissing you, I wanted to be sure you knew."

Marion said, "Okay." She put down the food and went to Sofia. They hugged, and Marion pressed her lips to Sofia's neck. "I appreciate how much it means for you to say those words to me. And maybe it's a call-and-answer because one person sometimes waits until the other person is strong enough to say it first, because they're worried about being blindsided."

"Maybe."

"I love you, too," Marion said.

Sofia closed her eyes and tightened her embrace. After a moment she pulled back and rested her hands on Marion's hips.

"Reggie and I had this thing... it was a silly little gesture. But we could do it in public, and it had this Pavlovian impact on me." She tapped two fingers against the back of Marion's hand: three taps and then brushing upward on the third tap. "I love you." She tapped again, three more times. "I love you."

Marion smiled. "I like that." She kissed Sofia and took a step back. "Should we get started on dinner?"

Sofia curled her fingers around Marion's hand. "In a bit... c'mon..."

"I really should get the sauce going first. It might take a while."

"So dinner will be late."

Marion smiled and let herself be pulled into the bedroom. She and Sofia may have had the rockiest start imaginable, and there may have been moments where they became bitter enemies instead of lovers, but she felt the pain and anguish was worth it for the end result. There would still be bumps in the road ahead of them. They would argue and butt heads and hurt each other's feelings. She was grateful for those confrontational early days because now she knew it was worth fighting through all of those obstacles if it meant she got to end the day with the most amazing person she'd ever known.

She smiled and joined Sofia on the bed and decided if they delayed too long for her to make the sauce, they could just order pizza.

EPILOGUE

SOFIA SAT in one of the red chairs at the Olympic Sculpture Park, a position not far from where she had met Reggie Mitchell eight, almost nine years earlier. Her hands were freezing because she didn't yet have a coffee to warm them up. She twisted at the waist and saw her deliverance arriving, a steaming cup in either hand. Marion smiled as she offered one of the cups to Sofia and then took the seat next to her.

"What a crazy coincidence, running into you here," Marion said.

"It's a small city. Everyone runs into everyone else eventually."

Marion said, "Yeah, but you and I are like magnets. Everywhere I go, there you are."

They drank together in silence, the chairs preventing them from touching. They rarely touched in public beyond a quick brush of fingers on a sleeve or an arm hooked casually around an elbow. Everyone in Sofia's circles knew that she considered Marion a friend, so it wasn't unusual to see her at Sofia's apartment or in attendance at a get-together. If anyone noticed that Marion seemed to linger until she was the only one left behind, no one said anything.

Sofia smiled as she took a sip of her coffee. "Mm. This is perfect. Thank you."

"You're welcome." She affected a posh accent. "It is my honor to provide the coffee for the reigning queen of Seattle news."

"Oh, god. Shut up."

Marion laughed. "As you wish, my Queen."

Her first few weeks in what she still considered to be Del's position had been a success. Ratings were originally on-par with a year earlier, but then began to tick up. She swore she wouldn't pay attention to numbers, that she only cared if they went down, but she felt a certain amount of pride that she might've had a small impact. The newspaper was the first to call her the Queen of Media, in which Marion took much pleasure. Not just because it was her MEOW user name but because of a certain game they'd played in the bedroom not long before the first story came out.

Sofia blushed at the memory and decided to change the topic. "It was right along here that I first met Reggie."

"Really?" She looked out over the harbor as if just noticing where they were. "It's gorgeous."

Sofia smiled and nodded. "It was insanely early. And raining. And she came walking along in a tuxedo and an Army jacket. She should have looked ridiculous, but... it was like she was waiting for the world to catch up with her. She was the only one dressed right and the rest of us were just too slow."

Marion chuckled. "What made you say something? Did you make fun of her outfit?"

"I would never."

"You would. You're a snob."

Sofia glared at her, playfully. "No. I asked if she was looking for a wedding. She asked if I was offering." Marion laughed, and after a moment Sofia joined her. "It was a good line, I admit."

"Yeah."

"She also asked, what if this is a story we tell our grandkids? The moment we met, on this sidewalk in the rain."

Marion said, "It still might be. Our story doesn't happen without Reggie."

"True. But if we start the story that far back, there are a lot of sad parts. Angry parts. Parts where I hate you. Parts where you can't stand the sight of me."

"Eh," Marion said dismissively. "Who cares? That just makes things interesting. The only thing that matters is that the ending is happy."

Sofia said, "Yes." She held her hand out palm-up. Marion

placed hers on top of it. They squeezed. "Thank you for being my happy ending, Marion Vogt. And my rage and frustration and everything in between."

Marion bent down and twisted their hands so she could kiss Sofia's knuckles. "Any time. Oh, I wanted to give you a present."

"A present? For...?"

"For because," Marion said. "Because I happened to think of it and didn't want to wait for a special occasion." She had taken out her phone and pressed her thumb against the screen until all the apps began to shake. She handed the device to Sofia. "There you go."

Sofia looked at the dancing apps. "And what exactly is this present?"

"I want you to delete the MEOW app."

"Really?"

"We've been together for a few months. We've said I love you to each other. We had that fight where I threatened to carve up all your clothes."

Sofia laughed.

"If we can get through that, then I don't foresee why I would need a dating app. So I'm letting you delete it. Ceremonially, as a grand gesture."

Sofia put her coffee on the ground and took out her phone. She made the apps dance as well before she handed it over. "At the same time?"

"One, two..."

They deleted the app.

Marion said, "I mean, our accounts are still there if worse comes to worst."

"Sure."

"Just in case."

"A safety net."

"Mm-hmm."

When they exchanged phones, Sofia tapped her finger three times against the back of Marion's hand. Marion smiled. "You too."

They settled into their seats and looked out at the harbor. There were ferries coming in from Port Townsend and the San Juans. They were getting good at finding moments like these, short stretches where they didn't have to worry about what they could or couldn't say because the silence was so easy and comfortable. They could have been close friends or strangers. No one had to know.

After a few minutes, Marion said, "Did she ever tell you why?" Sofia looked at her. "The tuxedo. Did she ever tell you why she was wearing it so early, in the rain? And where did the Army jacket come from?"

Sofia laughed and nodded. "She did. That morning, actually. It was the first conversation we ever had. I could tell you, if you really want to know. It's kind of long."

"Does it have a happy ending?"

"It ends with her meeting me."

Marion said, "Mm, good. That's my favorite ending. Go ahead."

Sofia smiled and began to tell the story.

"Once upon a time..."

Geonn Cannon lives in Oklahoma. He is the author of several novels, including the Riley Parra series which is currently being produced as a webseries for Tello Films, and an official Stargate SG-1 tie-in novel. Information about his other novels and an archive of free stories can be found online at geonncannon.com.

www.ingramcontent.com/pod-product-compliance
Lightning Source LLC
Chambersburg PA
CBHW071823190726
48292CB00005B/1575